THE ALIEN'S *DEFIANT* OMEGA

contents

one

. . .

BLAINE

Regret filled me as soon as I entered Mukhana's atmosphere.

I'd hoped to keep this planet in my rearview permanently. Now here I was, willingly returning to the place that had given me enough stress to age me another decade.

I sighed heavily as we touched down on the dusty terrain for the fourth time in my life, disappointment practically dripping off me at the fact that my rescue mission had ended with Alex running right back into his captor's arms.

"Stockholm," I mumbled under my breath.

Although, he had been assessed by professionals before being allowed to return. Still, it was a hard pill to swallow. The Alex I'd known for five years was level-headed, calm, and shy. Even months later, I found it hard to believe that he would run off to mate with an alien without some serious coercion.

I had to admit that the few times we'd spoken, he had seemed happy. Even with Saar growling possessively over his shoulder.

Well, I was about to see firsthand how Alex was doing here and how Saar was treating him.

"You good?" my pilot asked.

Glancing over at him, I forced a smile and a nod and stepped out onto the sand. The nassa hadn't bothered to set up anywhere to properly land. This was the repeated spot, in the desert but walking distance to their city. Maybe if humans kept coming and going, they would do it soon.

I cared more about preserving an ancient society like this one than I did about modernizing it. But Mukhana and I... we had a *history*.

The door sealed shut behind me, and I stepped back far enough for my pilot to fire the engine back up. This was just a drop-off since I was scheduled to be down here for a while.

I wasn't used to watching my only means of escape off planet leave me behind. After all these years doing this work, it was an isolating feeling to suddenly be stranded in the middle of a desert while my ship flew away.

As it rose above me, the oppressive heat of Mukhana enveloped me, and I turned my gaze down to the immediate surroundings.

The desert was bare and desolate.

Like all deserts, there was probably more life here than met the eye, but I couldn't see any. In all directions, there was flat earth, distant hills, and mushroom rocks eroded by wind into various interesting designs.

Then I caught sight of people approaching and realized they were coming from a large cluster of what I'd thought were dusty hills. I remembered thinking the same thing the first time I'd arrived here. From a distance, their city appeared not as buildings but as a natural part of the landscape.

On the other side of the city, I knew there was a mountain—I could almost see the ridges from here. Mount Ethos, Alex had written, where the bonding ceremonies were held.

His report on that aspect of the culture had been almost reverent and thinking about it now made my stomach drop all over again.

I walked toward those coming to greet me, nothing but a backpack slung over my shoulders, but then I stopped dead, realizing that one of those in the welcoming party was significantly smaller than the others in the group. My heart leaped as I realized it was Alex. He had come with the nassa to meet me.

Despite myself, a grin took over my face and my steps sped up.

It was only as we drew near that my steps faltered and I realized—it wasn't Alex. It was another human. I should have guessed when I didn't see Saar. I couldn't imagine the big brute allowing Alex out of his sight alone.

Disappointment filled me, but I schooled my features as the welcoming party drew to a stop before me.

I recognized all of them. They had come to meet us on that first disastrous arrival here. Head Alpha Kion—who was something of a chieftain by human standards with the rest acting as his council. His second, Alya, and one who I believed was Eisa. That explained the other human.

"Devin Hart?" I guessed.

"That's me," he agreed, reaching out and shaking my hand firmly.

When I looked around, they all smiled and nodded to me.

"Welcome back," Alpha Kion said pleasantly. As though him and the rest of the council hadn't literally manhandled me all the way back to the security crew and forced us off their planet.

Talk about traumatic first exposure.

But, for Alex's sake, I would play nice for now. With gritted teeth, I returned the nod.

"It's my pleasure," I replied.

Without any more preamble, the nassa all turned, leading us back toward the city, but Devin lingered at my side.

"Hm," he muttered as we began to walk, shooting me a quick glance, "it may be all the time I've spent surrounded by nassa lately, but you just *look* like an alpha to me. Weird."

"Really?" I asked, raising a brow. No one had ever described me as overtly macho before, and I'd assumed that's what being *alpha* would entail.

"I'm surprised," I admitted. "I mean, I'm more of a professor than I am a fighter."

I was downplaying the planet-trotting. I'd had some adventures and didn't entirely plan to stop, but lately, the idea of settling in one place, and taking up teaching full-time called to me more and more. I had a lot of wisdom to share.

That was part of the reason I now missed Alex so much. I hadn't realized how much I used him as a sounding board until he was gone.

Devin shrugged.

"Maybe it's just a confidence thing," he mused.

Suddenly, a large, green-scaled arm dropped around his shoulders.

I glanced up, meeting Eisa's poisonous green gaze. Everything about him screamed toxicity and it wasn't just because he was glaring daggers at me.

Pretending I didn't see the blatant hostility in his eyes, I gave him a pleasant smile.

"Eisa, it's been a while," I said casually. "How is the mated life going?"

He blinked, looking startled, and Devin had to bite back a smile.

"Good," he finally answered, as though guessing the solution to a math problem.

Devin patted his arm.

"So, you'll be taking over Alex's work?" he asked, turning back to me.

"That's the plan," I agreed.

My backpack was heavy with all the paperwork Alex had sent me. He'd had to scan through the console to send everything up and then I'd printed it all before coming down here. It was fun doing things the old-fashioned way but after thirty minutes carrying it all as we walked in the intense heat, I didn't know how people used to carry their books and paperwork to school. This stuff was *heavy*.

"So… how is Alex?" I asked, glancing at the group of them as we walked.

"Alex was very eager to come to greet you," Head Alpha Kion said, "but he is tired from the pregnancy and we insisted that he rest instead."

"Ah." So there was the answer to my true question. I couldn't imagine Alex not being the first to meet me. It would have taken a lot to stop him. Like a great big, golden alpha blocking the door…

"Alex has been hard at work here," Kion said.

"Yes, we have read some of his reports," Alya added. "He has a lovely way with words. Are you also gifted in the art of writing?"

I noticed all three of the aliens watching me curiously now.

"Uh. No, not really. I just take down information and make recommendations. Things like that."

"Ah. How unfortunate."

I glanced at Devin, who gave me an amused look, then leaned closer to me and spoke in a low voice.

"They take their arts very seriously here. Now that Alex has started writing about Mukhana and the nassa from an outsider's perspective, suddenly they think he's an artist." He grinned. "Alex is very embarrassed about the whole thing."

"He *is* an artist," Alya said solemnly.

I raised my brows in surprise.

I had been reading Alex's stuff for years now. Normally, there was a standard rhythm to it. We essentially had to follow a spreadsheet with the basic information and then expand on each point as we saw fit. There was room to go into details once we reached essay level, and being the first human to live on Mukhana, Alex had already gotten to that stage.

His essay on Mount Ethos was the first one he had released, and it was quite engaging, but I had been distracted for most of the read by the thought that he was writing from firsthand experience.

As we reached the outskirts of the city, I expected to be taken directly to the council building, but instead, I was pointed in the opposite direction, through the streets.

In this casual way, I was given my first proper tour of Diwan, the biggest city on Mukhana.

In the daylight, with the sun shining while everyone went about their everyday life, my opinion of the planet was immediately thrown for a loop. I was surprised to see families playing in front of their homes, people working on building infrastructure, others tending small gardens and friends and neighbors talking...

A lot of the things Alex had told me about the planet came to mind. He'd gone on about the rich culture and history and how lovely it all was.

Alex was a professional in our field. Now, with all eyes on him, his work was gaining a lot of interest from humans and non-humans across the universe. It wasn't that I'd doubted him, per se, it was just that I couldn't help but feel that he was seeing through rose-tinted glasses. He was obviously infatuated, *and* he was pregnant, which was a whole other can of worms.

"This is where I work," Devin said, gesturing to a large wall that was high enough, I couldn't see what was on the other side of it.

"What do you do?" I asked, curiously.

"I train omegas."

There was an obvious note of pride in his voice, but my stomach sank the smallest bit because well, it was behind a huge wall... I didn't know what he was teaching them, but the fact that they cared about keeping people out was concerning.

I shivered as I was reminded of the planet *Lycea*. It hadn't been the first time that I had been reminded of that godforsaken place and what had happened there. And I suspected it wouldn't be the last. Mukhana seemed determined to draw out every long-suppressed memory I had.

Luckily, I was drawn out of my thoughts when my guides slowed to a stop before a house, much like

9

the others, with a domed roof and open doorways and windows.

"Here is your home for the duration of your stay," Alpha Kion said.

"We hope that you like it," Alya added.

Surprised, I glanced around.

It was on a fairly lively street with what appeared to be a park for the children to play in. There were a lot of houses and nassa walking around, clearly enjoying the sunshine and the atmosphere. Some of them looked on with open curiosity, but no one approached.

I was shocked to realize that this house was no different from any of the others except that, apparently, it was *mine*.

"It's great," I said. "Thank you."

"You are most welcome," Kion said, smiling.

"Feel free to come to me if you need anything in the meantime," Alya said. "I live in that house with the blue curtains."

I glanced over, seeing the house she was pointing to, where pretty blue curtains were moving gently in the windows and doors. She was only a couple of houses over on the other side of the street.

"And we live just around that corner as well," Eisa added. "I have a few things to do, but later Alex shall come to collect you to give you a tour."

"Thank you," I said, relieved that I would see my friend soon. "I guess I'll just settle in until then."

He nodded and turned to Devin.

"Will you join me?" he asked, but Devin shook his head.

"No, I have a class soon."

"Very well," he said and to my shock, the alphas simply nodded in parting, welcomed me again, and *left*. They were really just dropping me into the middle of their lives like it was nothing. Like I was truly welcome.

It was so unusual for an alien species to do something like this. Normally visitors were treated as such. With care and consideration and suspicion.

I wasn't quite sure what to think of any of this.

"I've got a few minutes," Devin said. "Can I come in?"

Nodding, I stepped into the surprisingly cool air of my new house.

The stone and mud walls clearly helped to keep the temperature down, much the way it had been done in hot climates on Earth long ago. It was a relief to be in the cooler temperature while I took stock of everything.

Black curtains were hung up over my doors and windows. I pulled the one over the front entrance shut behind me and then went through the house, examining everything.

The house was very much like any other. It opened into a living room, with chairs and a long pillow along one of the walls. A fireplace was erected in the middle of the room with a smoke hole above. A pile of wood and starter lay in a basket next to it. The next room was a kitchen, I guessed, based on the cabinets and what appeared to be a counter and a bowl, which I presumed was for water. Off to the side, to my surprise, was an indoor washroom. There was only a hole in the ground to serve as the toilet with a basin, a mirror, and a lamp set on the counter. Still, I'd expected an outhouse, so this was a pleasant surprise.

The room after that was large and spacious with a comfortable-looking bed, already made, set against the back wall below the large window. There was also a rather beautiful dresser with a mirror on top. Everything in the house appeared to be made with care and the dresser was no exception. When I looked closely, it was etched with leaves and berries.

"There's a well on the corner, out there to the left," Devin said, gesturing. "You'll probably have to refill your bucket daily. For bathing there's a big communal bathhouse. Food in the market. Are you hungry now?"

I shook my head.

"No, I ate before we headed down. And I have a couple MRE's in my bag."

Devin made a noise.

"I don't miss those," he shuddered. "Glad my military days are behind me, to be honest."

I pulled off my backpack, letting it fall to the floor, and then perched on the edge of the bed, watching him.

He was a gruffer man than I had expected, with rough stubble on his face. He was shorter than me, but obviously worked out too, and there was a gentleness in his eyes and the welcoming way he smiled to soften him up.

"Has it been a big adjustment?" I asked.

"Oh yeah, but in the best way."

He must have seen the surprise on my face because he laughed.

"Not the answer you expected?"

I shrugged, rubbing the back of my neck.

"Well, to be honest, no. Going from being a soldier to being controlled by—I mean *mated to* an alpha here."

I grimaced at the slip up while Devin's grin grew.

"Hey, no one is used to following orders better than a soldier," he joked.

I winced.

"So, you don't deny it?"

"It's actually fine for me," he said honestly this time. "Mated omegas have as much free run as any alpha. Because our pheromones no longer get to the alphas."

"I see," I said. "So it's the unmated ones that have it rough."

I expected him to argue, but he pursed his lips and nodded.

"Yeah," he agreed. "To be honest, it sucks for them. But I'm doing what I can to help them out."

"Your classes?" I guessed.

He nodded enthusiastically.

"I'm teaching them self-defense," he said, and suddenly, I understood why he was so proud. "Hopefully it becomes the norm for the omegas to be strong. Give the alphas a reason to learn some self-control, right? And believe it or not, Eisa is my biggest cheerleader."

I remained dubious but forced a smile.

"You should come today!"

"Yeah? I *am* curious," I admitted. "Is that allowed?"

"I don't see why not," he said. "My dad comes to watch sometimes and he's an unmated alpha."

I *was* interested to see them in action.

"Alright, should I come now?"

"I just have to do some set up first," he said. "So maybe come by in about thirty minutes?"

I nodded, glad I'd have a minute to myself first.

I'd tried to adjust my sleep schedule on the way from Kryon, but a week hadn't quite been enough. I'd been there for nearly two months and had fully adjusted to their schedule.

Now, I could feel the jet lag sinking in. The best way to deal with it was to force yourself to stay awake until nighttime, but I crawled onto the luxurious bed anyway, setting a ten-minute alarm. There were all types of fabrics. Some were furry, some were silky, some cottony.

This whole experience, right down to the bedding, had been surprisingly welcoming.

But no matter what reception I was given, I could not deny the feeling that I still had niggling within me. That humans and nassa shouldn't mix.

two

. . .

LATIF

"I do not like what these classes are doing to you."

My al-mother's words were grating to my senses. I had to shut my eyes and take a quick breath to remain calm before turning to face her.

I had taken a lot from my al-mother. She was striking in appearance, with shockingly pale skin and nearly black-blue scales, eyes, and hair. I had taken her skin tone and colors, although my blues were slightly brighter. I had even taken the shape of her face and the tilt of her eyes.

On the outside, aside from my slender frame, I looked so much like my al-mother.

But I was an omega. And she would never understand what I was going through.

I did not want the fight training to be taken away from me. Luckily, I had spent my entire life keeping my frustrations to myself, so it was with practiced ease that a smile landed on my face as I met her gaze.

"They are just silly classes taught by a human, Al-mother," I said. "Please don't take them so seriously."

Al-mother's frown deepened but at that moment, my om-father entered, interrupting what was sure to turn into an argument.

"Are you ready?" he asked, then paused, looking between us.

I waited, holding my breath, for what Al-mother would say. She'd made it quite clear that she didn't like these classes. If she really did not want me to go, I couldn't exactly run there on my own, unattended, and Om-father would take her side.

"Have fun," she finally sighed, and all the air rushed back into my lungs.

"Let's go," I said at once, grabbing my bag and slinging it over my shoulder, then grabbing Om-father by the arm and practically dragging him out the door.

We had to move fast, before Al-mother changed her mind.

Om-father allowed me to pull him several feet from the door before hastily lifting a veil to cover me from sight.

Under the canopy that fluttered about us as we walked, he gave me a knowing look, but remained silent until we reached the omega path.

Luckily our home wasn't very far from it, and the moment we were within the walls, Om-father dropped the fabric.

Most unmated omegas were allowed to go places as long as they had an escort, but my parents were stricter than most. That was why I knew the old omega paths like the backs of my hands. They were still used but sparingly.

Apparently, these omega paths had been a lot more commonly used in the past, before things had become less strict. I couldn't fathom the rules being even *more* rigid. Even with things as they were now, it felt oppressive.

"What were you fighting about this time?" Om-father asked.

I thought about denying the argument, but his blood-orange gaze was fixed on me, sharp as always, and I could not bring myself to lie.

"I do not want to have an auction," I said quietly.

Om-father was silent for a moment.

"Then how will you find your fated mate?" he asked curiously.

"I do not want to," I informed him firmly. "I do not want a bonding ceremony. I do not want an alpha."

Om-father's brows lowered, but his steps did not falter, and I was struck with the realization that he was not at all surprised by the declaration. Even though it was outlandish, he seemed prepared for my words.

"I know it may seem scary to be mated to someone you don't know, but trust me, my love, you will be happy once it is done."

He reached out as we walked, allowing his arm to fall over my shoulders to give me a loving squeeze.

I remained tense, shoulders drawn up too high. My tail swung a little too sharply, accidentally smacking against his.

"Ouch," he hissed, drawing back.

"Sorry," I said at once.

He sighed.

"Your Al-mother just worries because... well, what would you do with your life, Latif?"

"I would do what I want!" I argued. "I don't need an alpha to live on my terms!"

He bit his lip, shooting me a glance.

"So you would be happy—"

"Helping other omegas," I supplied. "Working in the temple, protecting our cave, teaching others to defend themselves so that they too can choose what to do with their lives—"

"See, *this* is why your Al-mother doesn't like the fight sessions you are taking."

"Because I don't want to bond?" I demanded.

Heat was rising back up to the surface now, annoyance flashing through me. In front of Al-mother, I had to control it, but Om-father allowed me to be myself more and it was hard to hide my true self when I was with him.

"Because," he said gently, "you are not speaking like a nassa. You are speaking like a *human*."

I couldn't deny his words. Devin had changed my life. And I was glad he had.

"And what is wrong with that?" I asked quietly.

My feet slowed to a stop and Om-father paused too, turning to face me.

"What is so wrong with wanting to do what I want? To not being tied to someone that I did not choose?"

"It limits you," Om-father said softly. "That is what's wrong. You will never be able to truly live freely until you mate. You will always be behind walls and fabrics, hidden away... you have already been hidden away for too long. We selfishly wanted to have our little omega in our home for a little longer."

He smiled regretfully.

"In that time, you grew into your own adult, and now you deny the good things we want for you."

I did not know how to argue that. My hands were trembling at my sides.

Om-father did not seem to notice. He turned, continuing down the path, and I followed because I did not want to miss my class, but my heart ached as we went.

"If alphas here were like alphas on the human planet, perhaps things would be different," Om-father mused. "But let me tell you, being able to walk the streets without escorts, to dance in the middle of a celebration, to mingle with all nassa is an incredible feeling and one you will only get from bonding."

"I could just go outside without an escort," I said, voicing the thought that had been growing louder and louder over the passing weeks. "Who is to stop me?"

Om-father did not answer and when I glanced at him, for the first time, he looked angry. His jaw was clenched and red brows furrowed, but he did not speak.

As we drew close to the exit point that led to the

training field where Devin held his class, Om-father put a hand on my arm, stopping me from leaving.

"Tell me, Latif, is it the fight training that has you speaking so carelessly?" he asked.

I swallowed.

"If an alpha attacked me or tried to bond with me, I could fight them off now, Om-father. I'm one of the best in the class."

He squeezed his eyes shut.

"Goddess help me, your Al-mother was right," he sighed.

For a moment I thought that he was going to make me turn around and walk back. That mingling with humans was about to become a thing of the past, but then he let out another soft sigh and shook his head.

"Latif, you must erase those ridiculous thoughts from your head," he chastised. "I don't want to take this away from you because it has meant so much to you, but if you continue this dangerous line of thinking, you will not be permitted to continue."

I tried to calm the rising panic that filled me at that thought. I didn't think either of my parents knew just how much this outlet meant to me. Or how much it had saved me.

Before the human Devin flew into my life, small and unassuming and completely inspiring, I had been too unhappy to hope for anything good. Now, life felt like a long list of opportunities, ripe for me to pick.

But they did not know because they were stuck in their ways. The *old* ways.

Things were about to change.

And it was going to be *me* to change them.

I just... did not know how yet.

"Yes, Om-father," I said finally.

He searched my eyes for a minute, then threw the veil up around us to continue to the field. It was such a short distance, the cover was unnecessary... but I had to play by their rules for the time being, so I just pursed my lips and walked.

When we passed the gate, I was disappointed to see that I was late. Devin was already there, leading the rest of the class through a warm-up.

"I'll send your brother to pick you up," Om-father called as I ran to take my spot.

"I'm going to the bathhouse straight after!" I shouted back.

"He'll take you there!"

I was already falling into place next to Alil, settling on the ground next to him and joining in the leg stretches that Devin was showing us. The small human was sitting on his backside, bending nearly double to hold onto one foot, then the next, in a move that he hadn't been able to do a few months ago but now made us do at the start and end of each class. He lifted his head when I arrived.

"Glad you could make it," he said, smiling.

"Thanks," I returned, happiness flushing through me. I was still here. I still had these lessons. I could have cried with relief.

Then Devin got on his knees and leaned back, lifting his hips.

I couldn't help catching Alil's gaze, and we both giggled.

I loved seeing Devin do this one. He looked very at ease in this position, whereas our tails always seemed to be in the way.

"Make it work," he chastised in mock seriousness. He could never fully hide a smile.

Taking his order, I straightened, swung my tail to the side where it wouldn't be in the way, and then got back into the position, enjoying the stretch.

For a few more minutes we stretched while Devin asked everyone how they had been. Then we stood and started the funny jumps that got our hearts racing.

"Another five burpees!" Devin shouted.

By the time we were ready for the actual warm-up drills, all of us omegas were disheveled, breathless, and smiling.

"I'm going to show you a new takedown today," Devin said, and excitement bubbled in me. I loved putting my opponents down.

"Latif, do you want to be my guinea pig?"

I still did not know what a guinea pig looked like, but Devin had explained a while ago that it was some sort of small furry creature that could easily be manipulated, so I knew what he meant.

Grinning eagerly, I stepped to the front of the class and faced him.

Devin was short, only coming to just above my shoulder, but that didn't seem to matter when we faced off against each other.

Despite our size difference, he could easily beat me every time. I aspired to his level.

Slowly, he walked me through the new technique, flipping me onto my back softly but swiftly.

I laughed when I landed, looking up at the clear blue sky and shaking my head.

If I were to become half as good as Devin was, no alpha could snatch me away the way my parents feared they would.

He offered me his small strong hand, grinning down at me and helping me stand.

"Ready to try it on someone else?" he asked.

I nodded eagerly and went to Alil as everyone partnered up.

"He made that look easy," Alil grumbled as we struggled through the steps.

"He has more experience," I argued to my violet friend, but failing to take him down a moment later made his frustration contagious. Devin chose that moment to approach.

"You need to lean into the front leg," he told me, at once catching the issue. With his guidance, I went through the movement again and Alil landed flat on his back with me over top of him.

"Nice one!" Devin said.

I stood up, grinning triumphantly, but before I could offer to help Alil up, the softly blowing breeze carried the most startling scent to us and my entire body reacted.

A shiver traveled over my skin and my muscles seized in shock.

Every unmated omega on the field froze.

As one, we all turned, looking upwind.

A human I had never seen before walked up the field toward us. An unmated alpha.

He was only a small human. That was what I told myself. That it was nothing to be afraid of, but it was like watching an Essa snake stalking toward me.

I had caught the scent of many unmated alphas, but never without a wall or family member separating us. Never without an alpha present to protect me... Never from one stalking toward me so confidently, like his presence was nothing.

Devin didn't seem to notice what was happening, marching out to greet him and I realized suddenly that the humans *didn't* notice. They were different. They probably didn't realize how inappropriate this was or how my parents would revolt if they knew.

They chatted for a minute before Devin glanced back, finally seeming to catch that all of us had stopped and were watching in fascination.

"This is my friend Blaine," Devin said. "I thought he might like to watch the practice, if you don't mind."

When no one responded, he instructed, "Back to the combo." But still, no one moved, and his expression turned puzzled. "What's wrong?"

"He is," I volunteered, jutting my chin in the direction of the human *Blaine.*

They both seemed taken aback. Devin recovered first, his face turning red.

"I thought because he's human you would feel safe around him."

He was already nudging Blaine back the way they had come, but the other man was having trouble holding back a smile. He seemed to find it *funny*, and anger bloomed in my chest.

"Does this amuse you?" I demanded.

If anyone found out about this—if I lost these classes because of his carelessness—there would be consequences. I didn't know what I would do, but I would make him pay.

"No, it's not funny," he said, and his deep voice seemed to pierce me. "It's just—why would *you* be scared of *me*?"

He laughed, betraying his words.

"It seems you human alphas are just like the nassa ones," I found myself saying—nearly snarling from anger. "You think you can do whatever you want to us. Even come into our private training to mock us."

His dark brows shot up and he shook his head fervently.

"No, I wouldn't mock you," he started. "Don't worry, I'm leaving."

He gave Devin a look then, as though to say *I told you so.*

It was the type of face my al-mother would make when I made mistakes and, just like that, my irritation grew tenfold.

"Good," I muttered. "Because alpha or not, I could take you down."

Suddenly Devin started laughing hard, like I'd said something hilarious.

"Sure you don't want to try it?" he asked me, grinning.

Surprised, I looked at the human alpha.

Blaine shook his head, snorting.

"No, no, it's okay, I believe you. You win. No need to *take me down*."

The derision in his tone set me even more on edge.

"You don't think I can beat you?"

Despite every rule that said I should do the opposite, I stalked up to Blaine.

To my surprise, he wasn't as short as the other humans.

I knew I was small for a nassa, but when I realized that Blaine only stood a few inches shorter than me, my heart skidded to a halt.

He squinted up at me with eyes the color of a summer storm—just like the hair at his temples.

He opened his mouth and began to hold up his hands, perhaps in surrender, but without thinking, I reacted.

I reached out, swiftly moving through a wrist-lock takedown. My favorite of the ones I had learned so far, because the more your opponent struggled, the more it hurt.

I expected resistance, I expected him to know

some sort of retaliation, but Blaine just fell flat onto his back with me atop him, pinning him down.

He grunted in pain, and I immediately released him.

For a moment, we stared at each other, chests heaving. I could hear gasps and murmurs and someone laughing but could not tear my gaze away from the alpha under me.

"Damn," he finally muttered under his breath, "that was fast. Don't know why you're so worried about me being around. You can obviously take care of yourself."

Pride filled me at his unexpected words. I was so surprised that I could do nothing but stare down at his fascinating face.

He was so masculine. There was very little that was soft about him. His jaw was strong and covered in rough stubble. His eyes were sharp as claws. He had high cheekbones and even his hair was spike-straight, cut short like the humans seemed to favor.

And most interesting of all, he didn't seem bothered by the fact that I had bested him. He just looked at me, something like interest in his gaze.

"You don't mind that I won?" I asked. Hesitance and confusion tinted my voice. Then I had another thought that brought the frown back into place. "Or you don't think an omega is worth fighting, is that it? Are you mocking me?"

He smiled up at me playfully, and my stomach flipped.

"Trust me, I would not mock a muscular, seven-foot-tall alien on the best of days."

For a moment, I didn't know what to say.

"So you really do not mind losing to me?" I asked, confused.

"No," he chuckled. "You clearly know what you're doing, and I haven't a clue how to fight like this."

Finally, I remembered that we were not alone and looked up to find everyone watching us. Blaine followed my gaze, exchanging a look with Devin, who had to bite his lip to stop from smiling and even then barely managed to hide it.

He approached us, chuckling and I moved to release Blaine, suddenly realizing that I was strad-dling an alpha. And his body was hard and warm between my thighs, his scent suddenly all-encom-passing. If my al-mother could see me now...

I scrambled off of him, my heart thudding against my ribs as the reality of what I had just done hit me.

Devin offered Blaine a hand, helping him up with a sympathetic wince.

"You sure you don't want to learn a couple defensive moves before you go?" he asked, then glanced at the rest of the class. "Anyone else want a try with an actual alpha for practice? A safe one."

A couple of them looked interested, but no one spoke up and Blaine quickly jumped in.

"No, no, I got my ass kicked enough for one day."

"You think *that* was an ass-kicking?" Devin chuckled. "Latif can do way more than that if you let him."

Blaine glanced down at me, his gaze rapt.

"I'll bet he can," he said, and my stomach made that strange movement again, like I was about to jump from too high up.

"I'll get out of your hair," he finally said.

What a strange thing to say. My hair was tied back and he certainly had not been tangled in it. But Devin and Alex both said things that had different meanings, so I guessed he meant he was leaving.

Sure enough, he made a hasty escape.

"The human alphas truly are different," Samia, one of the younger omegas, said. "I don't believe that human would be unable to control himself the way a nassa alpha would be."

"No," Devin agreed. "For humans, it's more on a case-by-case basis what type of person someone is. Anyone can be an asshole, but he doesn't seem like the type."

He looked at me then, still sitting where I had landed on the ground after jumping from Blaine.

"You okay?" he asked.

I nodded quickly but didn't elaborate, bowing my head to avoid his gaze. How was I supposed to explain that my body had reacted to our position and that I could not stand just yet or everyone would know?

I bit my lip, embarrassment filling me, but luckily, without Blaine present, the feeling passed quickly, and my body began to calm down.

"I think we'll call it quits early," Devin said, "unless anyone wants to stay behind and keep working."

Normally I was the first to volunteer or beg for a few more minutes to practice a new technique, but this time, I shook my head, standing to collect my belongings for the bathhouse.

"I can't believe you did that," Alil whispered next to me, voicing my own thoughts.

"Neither can I."

three

. . .

BLAINE

My ego wasn't exactly bruised, but other things were. My wrist, in particular, was aching from the way that omega had folded it before twisting my arm.

I'd come directly back home, too tired to explore and despite myself, I crawled straight back into bed, still shaking my head over what had happened.

I wasn't inept when it came to fighting, but groundwork was my enemy and anyway, I'd meant what I'd said to the omega. I wasn't one to pick fights, not with guys that were bigger than me, and especially not over a misunderstanding.

I found myself smiling as I pulled the cover around me. There had been something sweet in the sincerity with which that omega had challenged me.

And what a beautiful person to get pinned under. God the nassa were attractive. And I'd learned today that the omegas were most of all.

What had his name been, again? Devin had said it...

Latif, I believed and murmured it aloud. It rolled off the tongue.

———

I woke up to Alex's cheerful voice. My eyes fluttered open. For a moment I was sure that the last few months hadn't happened and we were still on one of our last missions before ever coming to Mukhana.

Bromelia had been a fun planet to visit. Me and Alex had enjoyed climbing their tall trees and sleeping in their canopies for a few days. He'd joked that it was as close to a tropical vacation as we were ever going to get, and I had agreed.

"Blaine?!"

"In here!" I shouted groggily.

I was just forcing myself to sit up by the time Alex appeared in the doorway.

Still pregnant. The last few months really *had* happened, unfortunately.

That didn't stop a grin from taking over my face.

I could see his big smile before I took in anything else. He was walking a bit funny, waddling from side to side and he was bigger too, but as he reached the bed, I barely registered anything but his happy face. The expressive blue eyes that crinkled when he smiled, the full, wide lips, cheeks tinted pink from too much sun.

He sat to give me a big hug.

"Sorry I didn't come meet you!" he said. "Did you do anything yet?"

The look he gave me then said he expected a very specific answer.

Before I could guess, he burst into laughter.

"I heard you got your ass kicked by an omega at Devin's class!" he guffawed.

I grimaced.

"How do you already know that?"

"Word travels fast in Diwan," he chuckled. "Don't bother trying to keep secrets."

"Great," I chuckled, "I didn't take the nassa for gossipy neighbors."

"Oh they are," Alex said.

He couldn't stop smiling and was squeezing my arm warmly.

"I'm so glad you could come. It's so good to see you again."

"You too," I said, warmth flooding me. "You look—"

I faltered as my gaze landed on his belly.

"Like a buddha," he supplied, blushing and I guffawed.

"How do you walk?"

"Slowly," he admitted. "Have you settled in?"

I nodded. "Yeah. The time difference is the main issue. Tried to turn around my sleep schedule on the way here, but the week-long trip wasn't quite enough time."

Alex grimaced. "Aw. Well, think you can handle a tour?"

I frowned. "I'll be okay, you don't need to show me around. I'll just go for a stroll."

Alex frowned, glancing down at his belly briefly before fixing me with a look.

"Are you really trying to protect me from walking too much?" he asked and then, before I could answer, "That's such an *alpha* thing to do."

Alex knew me all too well. Being compared to the alphas here made my skin crawl, considering.

"Nope. I'm not. Do what you want," I said, climbing out of bed. "Show me all the way up a mountain. I'm sure you can rock climb right now, right?"

He grinned. "Uh-huh, best rock climber on the planet. Let's go."

We were both smiling as we left my new place.

Alex didn't seem able to contain his excitement. He started to tell me about everything we passed, down to the detail.

Apparently, the fountain had been erected in the town square when a drought had left the citizens on the verge of death many years ago. The entire community had erected it together with different people making different parts. That was why each stone looked different.

By the time we reached a large, bustling market, I felt like my head was spinning from all the additional knowledge.

"I'm impressed," I said. "When do you find time to sleep?"

Alex shrugged sheepishly. "I haven't been working too hard," he lied. "I just walk around and talk to people, and anyone who has a lot of knowledge on a subject ends up getting a proper interview."

We paused at a table with what I thought was jewelry hanging all over their canopy. On second thought, it made more sense that they were sun catchers.

"Pretty," I said, admiring a blue one. It had a polished stone in the center that was nearly clear, like glass dipped in blue ink. Around it, silver and gold had been manipulated into the most beautiful pattern of sunshine and sunbeams.

"Are you the artist?" I asked.

The nassa, a rather shy-looking young male, shrugged sheepishly. "Yes. Here."

He pulled the piece down and tried to press it into my hands.

"What? No. I was just looking—"

"I insist," he said, smiling happily when I grudgingly took the piece from him.

Up close, it was even more beautiful, and I spent a moment admiring it before realizing that I was being stared at.

The moment I met the artist's fuchsia eyes, he looked away.

"Another human on Mukhana... an alpha this time. It's so nice to have you both here. You are very beautiful to look at. Just like these suncatchers."

I was more than a bit surprised by that statement. No one had ever called me *beautiful* before. Rugged, yes. Handsome, yes. Once or twice, I'd even been called charming, but that was about it.

Not wanting to offend, I couldn't help exchanging a glance with Alex who seemed unperturbed. Clearly, he was used to it.

"Well, thank you for this," I said, then I looked the nassa over. He was dressed much the same way that Alex was, but even more decorated, glittering right down to the bangles on his ankles and rings on his toes. He was beautiful. Nearly as beautiful as Latif…

"Are you an omega?" I hazarded a guess.

He nodded, eyes widening.

"You mean to tell me you really *can't* tell?" he asked. "I'd thought that was a rumor."

I shook my head.

"No, I'm afraid not." His shock was rather adorable. "Are you mated then? Or single?"

His lips parted in a shocked expression that quickly turned into a flattered bat of the lashes.

"If I wasn't mated, I would not be out here," he informed me, smiling shyly.

"Of course," I said softly. Not until he had been mated. It was downright depressing. A fact that was hard for me to ignore. I couldn't help but wonder if Alex would really like it here so much if he hadn't been mated.

Alex gave me a look in between a grimace and a smile but nodded.

"The unmated omegas are kept apart," he confirmed.

Kept apart. What a diplomatic way to put it.

I thanked the omega for his gift once more, and we continued on our walk. I held the trinket up to the sunlight again, momentarily getting lost in the cobalt depths of the stone. It reminded me of something.

"It's not the best system," Alex admitted quietly as we walked. "But it sounds worse than it is. The unmated omegas still get to live lives, they go to classes, they have friends, and they learn skills like *that.*"

He indicated the suncatcher still hanging in my hands.

"They just don't have any freedom," I couldn't help but say.

Alex shrugged but didn't respond.

It was customary for us to leave things as they were, to observe without getting involved. We'd been on plenty of planets worse than this one before. And before Alex started working with me, I'd seen plenty more.

But this was the planet that Alex had decided to make his home.

It was always hard to turn a blind eye to oppressed members of society. The omegas here *were* kept controlled and isolated. They clearly were not permitted to be a part of everyday life until they were *mated*. And the thought that they needed a big, strong alpha to be out and about, made me *itch*.

"It's not all bad," Alex finally said. "The omegas here really stick together. We have our own things going on. There's an omega night planned at one of the restaurants in a couple weeks—"

"That you'll have to be escorted to?"

"Not me, but the unmated ones, yeah. We also regularly hang out at the bathhouse. There are no alphas in our section."

I found myself chuckling.

"Well, I'm sure they get escorted there too."

Alex stopped walking, forcing me to follow suit.

"You're normally not so judgmental of other cultures, Blaine... This isn't like you."

I froze at his accusation. Shame filled me because he was right.

But the way he had been kept here against his will, even if he was happy here now, it felt wrong to me.

And more than that, it put me in a position that I had never wanted to be in again. Powerless to help the people who depended on me until it was too late.

Mukhana *wasn't* Lycea, I reminded myself. Alex was okay. He had his reasons for liking it here. It was just hard for me to wrap my head around my dear friend choosing an alien he'd just met over the life and career he had worked so hard to build.

When he'd chosen Mukhana—when he'd chosen *Saar* over everything else, it had been hard to accept.

"I know it's difficult to understand," Alex said gently, "but being in a life bond with one of the nassa..."

He swallowed and then met my gaze, his own shining with determination to make me understand.

"It's like finding a part of yourself. It's *fate*. Being apart from Saar felt like I was missing my other half and, also, it almost killed him."

I stared.

He smiled sadly.

"I made it back just in time to save him," he said. "And I would do it again. I'm really happy here."

I bit back the rush of emotions that hit me. Not least of which was an overwhelming sense of rejection.

I'd had more than enough chances to make a move on Alex. At times, he probably would have gone for it. We'd spent countless nights in bars on other planets drinking and talking and getting loose in between work. We'd shared rooms and slept near each other under the stars...

Things had always been civil and easygoing

between us because we were colleagues. The few times I'd let the thought cross my mind of something more, I'd rationalized that it would be a bad idea to try to get intimate with someone I worked so closely with.

Why had it taken Alex being kidnapped for me to want to jump in...? Right when it was too late.

I had no one to blame but myself.

And I had completely accepted that it wasn't going to happen, but I still felt the oppressive need to care for him. After all, I had been his mentor for years.

Taking a deep breath, I tried to release those thoughts. I was sure I could work through once I had seen that he truly was happy here and that the omegas were okay. He was right, of course; it wasn't me to judge the way I had been.

I managed a smile.

"Let's start fresh," I suggested. "I'm here to learn about this planet with you. Not to judge it... I'm sorry I've been a bit of an ass."

Alex smiled warmly.

"It's forgotten. Come on, let's go meet Devin and eat."

———

Sitting on the floor on cushions around a table in a restaurant in Mukhana, I hadn't heard the end of my "fight" with Latif. The friendly banter, getting ribbed by an ex-military man and an old friend, had helped to make me forget that I had an issue with this place.

I paused, feeling the heat of the day already, and left a few more buttons on my shirt undone.

I was in shorts for once, a t-shirt, and comfortable shoes. I couldn't remember the last time I'd been so casual while on a mission, but this one was more of a favor than an actual work assignment.

Alex's research was spread out over the table I'd adopted as my desk. I'd spent most of the night reading it before passing out.

"Hello?" someone called from the doorway.

I recognized Saar's voice at once. Shit. It seemed that he was going to join us today. Honestly, I was surprised he let Alex go around with me the day before without chaperoning him then too.

Sighing, I went to the front curtain, opening it to find Saar standing before it with his arms crossed, waiting for me. I would have said hello if not for the glare. Instead, I crossed my own arms in return and lifted my chin to meet his angry expression.

"Where's Alex?" I asked.

Saar's jaw twitched.

"He is too tired to join you today. Yesterday's events wore him out."

"Ah. I see..."

We stared at each other for a beat, but Saar didn't appear to be planning to break the silence *or* leave.

"Is he okay?" I finally asked.

"He is near the end of a pregnancy," he informed me coldly. "If you did not notice. He cannot be your tour guide while you are here. He has other matters to attend to, such as his health."

I grimaced, partially because it sounded like he had pushed himself too much and the idea of him doing that on my behalf did bother me. But also, Saar was as much a dick as ever.

"Alex seemed fine yesterday," I informed him. "I didn't even notice him getting tired."

"That does not mean—"

"I don't need a tour guide, either," I interrupted. "I have free reign of this place, right?"

It took a moment, but eventually, Saar nodded.

"Great."

I forced a smile.

"Thanks for letting me know," I added.

Saar stared at me for a long moment.

"Are you sure you don't require accompaniment? Alex told me to take you wherever you want to go."

He didn't even seem too bothered by that idea.

Apparently, Alex had the big guy as wrapped around his finger as it was the other way around.

"Thanks for the offer," I finally said, "but I'll be fine."

Saar nodded.

"Very well. If you need anything, don't hesitate to contact us. Any of your neighbors will be able to point you in the direction of our house or the council building."

"Noted. Thank you, Saar."

He nodded in return and turned, departing back down the street.

It was relatively quiet today compared to when I had arrived the day before. There was only one family playing with their children at the playground across the street. Aside from them, everyone was probably sleeping in.

For a moment I stood there, wondering what to do next.

I could finish going through Alex's work so far. Or I could pick up where he was wanting me to.

He had been on the verge of deep-diving into the omega lifestyle on Mukhana. He probably had a bit of a handle on it already, being one himself.

From what he and Devin had been saying yesterday while we ate, they had a bit of a friend group here already. The omegas stuck together, as did the alphas. Neither of them seemed to mind much and it seemed like they did enjoy living here, but it still left a bitter taste in my mouth.

As for me, being an alpha, I wasn't sure what exactly Alex had expected me to be able to do for him. If I got the same reception going around to the omega places today as I did yesterday, I wasn't sure that I would be able to do *any* of the research he'd wanted me to do.

I was probably better suited to collect information on the alphas, but then again, maybe they kept everything out in the open. Maybe that was why accessing the omega secrets was such a big deal to him.

But the idea of not even trying, of his research having to be put on hold because he was having a baby, bothered me for his sake.

And even though it made me feel a little guilty thinking about it, I wanted to see for myself just how much freedom, or lack thereof, they really had here.

Quickly, I went back inside and grabbed my notebook.

It had been a long while since I had been forced to use pen and paper, but it felt good to hold it in my hand for once instead of smooth glass, so I didn't complain.

There was a short and vague to-do list that I'd

copied down. On it was to discuss the nassa religion with the priest at the omega temple and to tour it, to do the tour of the omega caves, and to compile the info Alex had learned on omega upbringings.

His notes were unorganized but clear enough for me to decipher after all of our years working together. If I didn't have any luck with the rest, the least I could do was compile it all, but on only my second day on a new planet, I had no intention of staying in, poring over a desk piled with paperwork.

Tucking the notebook into my pocket, I stepped out into the sunny morning, suddenly excited to explore.

Diwan City had a side to it that I hadn't imagined. Bright colors spread out over beige stones on long, hidden paths, glittering glass, and stone displays that sparkled when the sun hit them. And the people were just as colorful. Their scales shone as brightly as their polished stones. There didn't seem to be reason for their vibrantly hued tails and hair and eyes, although genetics played an obvious part. I stared with interest at a little girl tinted a lovely indigo whose parents were red and blue respectively.

They took a minute to chat to me about it, thanking me afterward for taking the time to speak with them.

Being a human on a planet like Mukhana was almost like being a celebrity.

Everyone wanted to talk to me and, as I had very little else to do, I took the opportunity, asking questions and getting to know the locals.

By the time I followed the sound of rushing water to reach a large, breathtaking building with massive pillars and overall impressive architecture, I grudgingly understood why Alex and Devin were so at home here already.

"That's the omegas' entrance," someone told me.

I paused and looked at the older man, who smiled down at me. He had silver spikes running over his shoulders and I'd gathered that only the alphas had those.

"The alphas' entrance is this way," he said.

I followed him inside, shocked to discover that a massive waterfall poured through the center. I hadn't realized that sound had been coming from within.

"Come to the hot pool," he invited.

I followed him there, leaving my clothes on the shelf next to his and taking a spot in the warm water.

I let out an appreciative sigh.

There were other alphas in the hot pool, watching me with open interest.

"Do you have anything like this on Earth?" one of them asked.

"Oh, definitely," I said. "Nothing that I've ever *seen*, of course."

That drew a couple of chuckles.

Despite myself, I returned the open looks that the other alphas gave me. It was interesting how coed everything was here. Females and males sat naked all around me, but none so much as glanced at each other. Everything was based on their *other* designations.

Yet children seemed to have free reign.

"When do you find out if you're alpha or omega here?" I asked, curiously. "Does it just develop one day?"

"Oh, no," the female alpha next to me said, smiling. "We can always tell, but it does not become an issue until our children go through puberty."

"That makes sense," I mused.

They were like humans in that sense. It was when they developed that everyone started thinking with their downstairs brains.

"Do you really not know who is an alpha and omega?" the young male on my other side asked.

I shook my head. "No, not at all."

"How do you know who to be with then?" he asked, looking confused. "Do you have auctions?"

I shivered at the reminder of the *auctions,* as they called them. That day, when Alex was about to be sold to the top fighter... I'd been sick to my stomach. I hadn't slept a wink until I got to talk to him again, and by then, just as I'd feared, it was too late.

I had to swallow down the memory to answer him.

"No, we just base it on who we're attracted to," I finally said. "And if they're interested as well, then we move forward and see how it goes... I mean, that's mostly how it is. Earth has a lot of different cultures, but for me, that was always how it was."

They all stared at me. Then the youngster broke the silence again.

"You mean to tell me that you've had... intercourse?" he asked, voice hushed and eyes wide as saucers.

I almost laughed and then had to stop myself as I glanced around. They all looked shocked. Just like that day in the council building, when I'd mentioned kissing people. At the time, I'd just thought they were extremely conservative. Now it clicked.

It wasn't that they *didn't* get intimate, was it?

"You... *can't*, can you?"

"Not unless we are bonded," the older man said.

Alex had been keeping a certain aspect of the nassa completely off the page, it seemed.

I shook my head. All this time, I'd thought the alphas were asshole rapists around the omegas. They were all terrified of getting attacked and stolen, weren't they?

I scratched my head in confusion.

"So... why are omegas kept separate then?" I asked, unable to help myself.

"Their pheromonal scent is irresistible to us," one answered. "It's for their own safety."

Suddenly, it struck me. The fear was over the bond. And why wouldn't it be? They would be stuck with some alpha forever and had no say in the matter whatsoever.

I had to bite my tongue to stop from saying what I wanted to—that alphas should be taught to control themselves. That keeping omegas hidden from view wasn't the answer.

And no one seemed to have any insight on the matter. They were too used to it. But maybe someone like the temple priest would have more to say.

"Do any of you know the way to the omega temple?"

four

. . .

LATIF

I stepped into the cool sanctuary of the omega temple and did not look back at Al-mother, who had escorted me here with an iron grip on my bicep.

My jaw was still clenched hard enough that it was starting to hurt, but I couldn't release the tension that was running through my entire body.

The temple was set high up on a hill with steps on all four sides, so that alphas would think twice about coming up here. If the long walk to the jungle wasn't enough to deter them, I doubted that some stairs would. No, to me it was yet another form of seclusion. Just another way that omegas were kept apart.

Even though there were more pillars than walls, it still felt that way.

Up high, we could see only into the thick trees and watch the path leading to us from above. I did not want to watch my al-mother's retreat, so I stepped into the back room, sealing myself off from the rest of the world.

The walls here had cutouts in the stone to let the light through in lovely lattice patterns, but at least I could let my guard down a bit.

I let out the deep breath that I had been holding, my eyes fluttering shut as I allowed the feeling of doom to collapse around me.

"Oh, Latif. You are here early," someone said behind me.

I jumped, turning to find Naz sitting on the bench behind me, one of his large tomes open in his lap.

He was always in here reading. I should have known.

"Hello," I said.

He patted the spot next to him, and I approached, sinking into the seat.

"What has happened?" he asked. "You look as though the world is crumbling."

I tried to smile but couldn't.

"Did you hear about what happened yesterday?" I asked.

He shook his head, and I snorted.

"Well, it seems like you are the only one who the gossip didn't reach yet."

He waited, not pushing me or reacting to my words.

"I got into a fight with an unmated alpha."

Now his eyes widened.

"A physical fight?" he asked.

"Yes," I admitted, and my lips betrayed me with a smile I couldn't hold back. "And I won."

Naz stared for a moment and then slowly smiled in return.

"Interesting," he said.

Finally, he shut his book. Instead of setting it next to him, he stood and returned it to the spot it belonged on the large bookshelf before turning to face me thoughtfully.

"You always were a little bit different, Latif... You remind me of myself."

I arched a brow, surprised by the priest's words. He was a quiet recluse who lived in the temple. I was a little too outspoken and prone to fighting for the chance to... *do things my own way*, I realized.

Naz must have seen the moment understanding lit my eyes, because he smiled and nodded.

"The reason you chose to be a priest," I guessed.

"It was something that I could choose to do on

my own. I live life how I want now. I never mated, even though there are plenty of alphas who would try to have me."

His gaze turned to the light pouring in through the wall and the city beyond.

"With the birthrate of omegas dwindling, some consider it a disservice to not bond. But just because things are changing, does not mean we owe our bodies and our freedom to make them stay the same."

I swallowed.

"Priest," I whispered, "if my al-mother knew you were saying things like this, I would never be allowed back here."

He chuckled.

"Your Al-mother is not unique in her ideals. No alpha would agree with me," he said. "That's why they are not allowed up here. This is *our* place, and it is safe here, to do and feel however you do."

I shook my head. If everyone could just acknowledge and respect how smart and capable omegas were, I felt like things would be different. Just because we weren't made for fighting the way alphas were did not mean anything. Omegas had no claws or fangs, our backs weren't spiked, and our tails weren't venomous. We weren't made to kill, but we didn't need to be. Even our one failing could be rectified with Devin's training. When all the omegas could hold their own against any alphas, what would they have over us?

"You know, the alpha I fought with was human. It seems like they are very different there," I mused.

"How so?" Naz asked, interested.

"He did not know how to fight," I chuckled. "And he did not seem to care. Being bested by me did not bother him."

Naz's auburn brows rose.

"Truly?" he asked.

I nodded.

"Even though he smelled so much like an alpha, he did not behave like one."

"Was he not affected by your scent?"

"I don't believe he smelled it."

"Wow...," Naz breathed. "I wonder if human omegas know how lucky they are."

I wondered too. The only human omegas I knew were mated to nassa alphas. I didn't know how they had been so unlucky, but they did both seem to be happy, so I kept my judgment to myself.

And of course, the only alphas I really knew were my mother and brother. They were not the best example for me. Although I loved them both, they were suffocating to be around.

"If only they would meet the human," I sighed.

"They would realize it was harmless. Inappropriate, perhaps, but harmless. He did not carry me away or try to kiss me. He did not try to touch me at all."

"I admit, now even *I* would like to meet him. I cannot imagine an alpha like that."

"Well, on Mukhana, I'm afraid he is one of a kind. Not that that stopped my parents from banning me from Devin's classes."

I pushed abruptly to my feet, trying to shake my frustration away. I would not let it go without a fight. Once they calmed down, I would try to reason with them again.

"I will clean the floors today," I said, and Naz nodded.

Although I volunteered here weekly, he did not ever tell me what needed to be done, allowing me to decide. Perhaps that was his small way of allowing us unmated omegas to have some autonomy.

I smiled, warmed by the realization. Just as I reached the door, Naz stopped me.

"What about you?" he asked. When I met his eyes, they were sharp with interest, boring into me. "Did *you* react to the human alpha the way an omega would?"

For a moment, I couldn't find my voice, and understanding passed through Naz's gaze.

"I didn't do anything—"

"I understand," Naz interrupted. "Just because your body may react, doesn't mean that you will act on it. We practice self-control at all times. Omegas are stronger than alphas in that way."

I nodded, embarrassment flushing through me even though he was being nice about it.

Quickly, I grabbed the brush, mop, and bucket of cleaner from the closet and went to work.

The fact of our biology had kept me up at night on more than one occasion. Alphas couldn't resist omega pheromones and acted on it by bonding to them, but they could not use their bodies in that way until the bond was done.

Meanwhile, omegas could get aroused and there was nothing like the scent of an unmated alpha to set one off. I'd never been so hard as the time an alpha had passed my bedroom window early one morning. I still remembered shamefully rutting against my bedding, unable to help myself before remembering self-control.

I shivered at the thought.

It was like our very bodies were pushing us to give in to an alpha to meet those needs.

And that thought scared me so much that I knew I never would. How could I trust that I wasn't acting based on my body's desires?

Having Blaine under me was already closer than I

was ever going to get to making love. I had already decided that years ago.

My family wanted me to have an auction. And soon. Om-father kept saying things about how the winner was decided by fate and would win no matter what. He kept saying how happy I would be to be with my soulmate.

But, if that was true, the unfortunate alpha was going to have to live life without me, because I wouldn't do it.

Sweeping and mopping the large stone temple, my thoughts finally began to clear.

I would find a way to wear Al-mother down...

I was sweating as I finished the last strip of floor, coming to the edge of the steps that led to the top and the strangest feeling hit me, like I was suddenly reliving yesterday for a split second. An alpha's scent carried on the wind toward me. *Blaine's scent.*

I froze for a moment as it enveloped me. Then I turned, looking down the stairs, sure it couldn't be, but there he was.

My breath caught at the sight of him.

He was standing at the bottom of the staircase, still wearing the strange human clothing that seemed to hug all of his limbs. This time, his legs and arms were exposed. His short hair hung into his eyes as he looked up at me, meeting my gaze.

As though it was nothing, he grinned and waved.

"Fancy running into you again," he called up.

Unsure what to say, I stared down at him.

It looked like he had made some friends, because he was with two other alphas. Their scents reached me too. One mated, one not. Both of them should have known better than to come here. Even standing and gawking from the bottom of the steps was inappropriate.

"Latif!"

Naz's voice hissing for my attention had me turning, catching him waving me over from behind one of the pillars.

Coming back to reality, I hurried to take shelter where Naz was hovering.

"Is that him?" he demanded anxiously. "What are they doing here?"

"I don't know," I said, leaning to look, but Naz tugged me back before I could see more than Blaine's broad back as he was speaking to the others.

"Are they coming up?" he asked.

I placed a hand on his arm, trying to calm him.

"They *wouldn't*," I assured. "The human alpha is harmless anyway, like I told you. He doesn't seem to be very aware of the rules here. After all, he walked into a training field of all omegas without thinking it would be an issue."

Naz's lips twitched.

"It's more the other one I'm worried about."

This time when I leaned around the pillar to look, Blaine was standing there alone, simply looking up at the building with interest.

"The nassa alphas left," I said, and despite—or maybe *in* spite—of what my parents would think, I stepped out into full view again.

"What do you want?" I called down.

Blaine grinned at me.

"Just to accidentally cause havoc wherever I go, apparently."

I frowned down at him.

"I met those two earlier and they wanted to show me around. Alex asked me to talk to the priest here so I thought I would stop by, but I don't think it's going to work out how he wanted it to."

He shrugged helplessly.

"Nice to see you again," he added as an afterthought. And apparently that was meant in parting, because he turned to head back toward the path. To my surprise, Naz stepped out from behind the pillar to stand next to me.

"I am the priest," he said. "Where is Alex?"

Blaine turned back to face us, his eyebrows arched.

"He's not feeling great," he said. "He wanted me to take over some of his research."

He glanced around, his hands tucked in his pockets, then looked up at us again.

"May I come up?"

Naz gave me an incredulous look.

"See?" I muttered. "He hasn't a clue."

Naz's lips quirked, but he forced them into a frown before looking down at Blaine.

"Alphas are not permitted in the temple," he said.

"Ah. Figured as much," Blaine sighed.

"But wait there, we are coming down."

Shocked, I stared at Naz.

"You said you easily fought and defeated him, did you not?" he asked in a hushed voice. I nodded quickly. "Then you can act as my guard."

Taking my arm in his hand, he led me down the steps, straight toward the alpha. My heart raced in a giddy way, like we were doing something naughty.

Naz stopped us a few steps above Blaine, keeping some distance between us and looking down at him curiously.

"You smell very potently like an alpha to me," he said. "Do you really not smell our pheromones?"

"Afraid not," he said. "I'm sorry to say that the only way I can tell you apart from alphas is the lack of weaponry on your shoulder blades."

Naz watched him for a moment, searching his face in wonder.

I understood completely. It was disconcerting to be face to face with an alpha and have them be completely nonreactive to an unmated omega.

"You still are not permitted to enter this temple," Naz finally said. "Only omegas may cross the threshold."

He grimaced.

"I guessed as much," he said. "I'm afraid I came to Mukhana for nothing."

"Oh?" Naz asked.

He had a talent for making people talk, it seemed, because Blaine immediately explained.

"Alex wanted me to take over his research. He was at the point of delving into some of the omega history. He thought it would be okay for me, being human because I won't react to pheromones, but of course, it's cultural too that alphas aren't allowed to mingle with omegas."

"They *are* allowed," I argued. "They can go in the caves and on the paths and everything. As long as the omegas are mated. Neither of us are, so you'd best run off before you're spotted here and get me into even more trouble."

Blaine fixed his gaze on mine narrowly.

"I'm sorry," he said slowly, "but how did I get you into trouble?"

"Because of our fight, I'm no longer allowed to go to Devin's classes," I snapped.

His gaze narrowed further.

"The way I remember it, *you* attacked *me*."

"Because you—you shouldn't have been there! What were you thinking walking into a group of omegas like that?"

He held up his hands.

"Like I said, we were mistaken and I apologize."

He backed up a step, waving me off.

"And I'm going to take your advice and get out of here before it gets any more serious."

"Wait," Naz said, stopping him in his tracks again.

The priest's gaze flew between us several times before he finally fixed them on me and spoke.

"Perhaps you can be the answer to each other's problems."

"I don't understand," I said, frowning and Naz reached out, taking my hand and squeezing it.

"Blaine," he said, turning his round eyes to him. "Perhaps Latif can take you to the other omega sanctuaries. The ones you want to enter allow alphas."

"Mated ones," I argued. "And even if I *could*, why would I?"

"Latif. Think about it. The mated alphas are permitted within because they are no danger to the omegas. This human alpha is clearly different than our own. If your Al-mother were to meet Blaine, your family might understand, don't you think?"

My heart leaped.

"They might let me take my classes."

"Perhaps it is worth trying. After all, you are the only omega that I know of who can fully defend yourself."

I glanced down at Blaine, suddenly desperate to make the man agree. If not for my entire life's worth of propriety instilled all the way into my bones, I would have rushed down the last few steps to grip his hands and beg.

But his scent was too overpoweringly alpha for me to ignore, and I remained stuck to the floor where I stood.

I swallowed, hoping that my eyes said it all.

"I would really appreciate it if you would," I managed.

He opened his mouth. Based on his expression, an argument was clearly on the tip of his tongue.

"I'll do anything you ask," I interrupted. "I'll take you wherever you wish to go. Answer any questions you have, just... *please*? All my parents care about is finding me a mate. They want me to have an auction and do nothing that is important to me."

I saw the moment he broke.

His shoulders sagged and he looked up to the sky as though asking the powers that be for strength.

"And you just want me to meet your parents in exchange?" he asked.

I nodded eagerly.

There was a good chance that this would not work. An even better chance that Blaine was about to get a good strike across the face. I shivered at the thought of what my brother would do if he saw me standing next to Blaine, but there was no way around it.

I had to try to make this work.

five

. . .

BLAINE

"You will stand on the other side of that tree until I make it clear that you should emerge," Latif ordered. "I will wait here. That way, you will have time to run should you need to."

I held back an eye roll.

If someone could explain to me why I was going along with this and putting myself in the position to possibly be attacked by overprotective nassa alphas, that would be great, because I had no idea.

Then Latif fixed me with those anxious blue eyes again and, this time, he bit the corner of his lip while staring at me.

"Thank you," he whispered.

And there was my answer.

Apparently, I was as weak to a pretty face as I'd always been, but really, how the hell was I supposed to say no to *that*?

Sighing, I looked over at the spindly tree that he expected me to disappear behind. Rude. The thing was only about six inches thick, and I wasn't a small guy by human standards.

Still, for some reason, I walked over to it and went behind it, turning sideways to buy a couple of inches.

"Oh good," Latif breathed. "Om-father came instead of my brother Addy."

I leaned around the tree, trying to follow his gaze.

Around one of the street corners, a fiery orange nassa omega was approaching. He looked nothing like Latif but was beautiful in his own way. His blood-orange hair was pulled back and tied up high, and his deep red robes swished as he walked. He had an air of elegance that just flowed naturally.

Clearly, Latif hadn't taken after his omega father in any way. He was brash in a way that I hadn't seen in any other omegas yet. Even now, he fidgeted anxiously.

His father paused in front of him.

"What happened?" he demanded at once, obviously able to read his son.

Unable to play it cool, Latif's gaze flew to me. Our eyes caught, his filled with dread that made my heart rate spike.

Of course, his father glanced over and saw me at once.

He froze and then, in full defense mode, marched toward me.

"You!" he shouted. "What are you doing loitering here?"

I stepped out, raising my hands in surrender.

"What are you doing at the omega sanctuary?" he demanded.

"Maybe you should ask your son," I said, and he swung around at once, not looking surprised.

"Latif!" he shouted. "Explain!"

Latif visibly cringed.

"I—I thought you should meet him to see—he's not dangerous."

His father gaped for a moment.

"Latif," he said again, exasperated this time, "don't tell me this is over those classes."

"It's not," he argued at once, "but surely you can see there's no reason for me to stop going. Perhaps you can convince Al-mother."

Suddenly, his father noticed the priest standing at the top steps, watching the show.

He gaped.

"Priest Naz," he said, sounding disappointed, "don't tell me you helped to arrange this?"

Naz grimaced and came halfway down the steps. He lowered to perch on them and smiled.

"Don't be too angry," he said. "The human alpha came here over a misunderstanding. It was fate that Latif happened to be here."

"Fate?" his father choked.

"Oh yes," Priest Naz said. "Why else would he arrive here right when Latif was volunteering? Something he only does once each week. And I am sure you can see that he is different than our alphas."

Latif's father stared.

"Blaine here needs an escort to some of our omega locations, and his friend is unable to guide him."

"And you expect me to allow Latif to be the one to do it?" he demanded.

"Why not?" Priest Naz asked. "Your son wants to, and Blaine cannot sense our pheromones."

Latif's father's gaze flew to me in surprise.

"It's true," I said, going for lighthearted. "And I keep accidentally getting into these situations. So it would be great to have someone who knows the place at my side."

Apparently, my easy attitude worked, because the tense line of his shoulders relaxed, before he frowned.

"Truly?" he asked. "You can't sense us at all?"

I nodded.

"Humans don't have that ability. And your son can easily beat the crap out of me, so you have nothing to worry about there," I chuckled.

He frowned.

"It's still extremely inappropriate," he said.

I winced.

"Well, I'd like to avoid it too. Just saying that *if* I happened to try anything on him, he would probably knock me out."

Still frowning, he looked between us all.

"Please Om-father," Latif begged, but he shook his head.

"I cannot allow it."

"What if… I convince your son to enter the auctions?" I asked.

Both of their gazes flew to mine in shock. Even I was surprised that I'd said it. I hated the tradition. But Latif wanted his training so badly and the fact that he asked for so little reached something inside me.

He deserved to go to his classes. And I hadn't given a guarantee.

But I might as well have, because hope filled his father's eyes.

"Yes," Latif suddenly said. "I will discuss it with him and hear his reasoning for me to do it. Once this is all over, I will even talk to you and Al-mother about it."

His father gasped.

"You will?" For a long moment, he searched Latif's face. "That changes everything."

"I will *talk* about doing it. I didn't say that I *would* do it."

His father's lips pursed.

"Well, it's not just up to me. Let us see if we can convince your mother and brother... It might take more than just talking. It might take promises."

Latif nodded resolutely.

His father turned and looked at me.

"I hope you are ready to face two headstrong alphas," he said.

"Right now?"

Honestly, the jetlag was kicking in, and I was ready to crash again. Not to mention that this had been dramatic enough for me already. I didn't exactly want to fight anyone.

"After we talk to them," he corrected. "Where are you staying?"

At my blank look, he waved me off.

"I will ask around and come collect you when it is time."

I forced a smile and a nod and watched them go.

Latif's father put an arm around his waist, leading him away, but before they got too far, Latif looked back at me over his shoulder, giving me an excited and grateful smile.

I sighed.

All this was for Alex, I decided. For some reason, the idea of returning to him empty-handed, when he had personally requested me to come help him, made my stomach hurt. I didn't want to disappoint him.

I would go into the omega cave he couldn't handle right now. I would take pictures and make notes so that we could pore over them together. Then, when he was back on his own feet, baby in arms, he could go and double-check my findings.

"That was kind of you," Priest Naz said, making me realize that he still stood there, watching me with those thoughtful eyes.

I shrugged.

"Thanks for your help," I said, stifling a yawn. "Now, if you'll excuse me, it's time to find my way back to my new bed."

That didn't turn out to be a problem. The moment I asked a nassa if they knew which direction to head, I was being led through the streets, back toward my place while the nassa happily chatted away. The fact that they all seemed to know where I was staying wasn't surprising. They seemed to have a close-knit community. Universally, that went hand in hand with gossip.

Not to mention that the nassa seemed to find it delightful having humans around.

As I reclined gratefully into bed, I wondered what we looked like to them. They seemed to find us *cute*. I shook my head, smiling ruefully at the thought. I would bet no one had thought that of me since I'd reached adulthood, and that felt like eons ago.

Now, in my early forties with a plethora of life experiences in my back pocket, the idea of continuing planet-hopping sometimes seemed *exhausting*. But I'd chosen this life a long time ago, and I didn't know what I would do if I stopped now. Even if it came with big aliens thinking I was a cute, harmless, little human.

I chuckled. They were probably right.

My mind traveled to one of my first jobs, one I hadn't remembered in ages. I'd been helping to acclimatize the human diplomats stationed on a planet where the aliens were fond of giving me little treats every time they saw me.

I shut my eyes, almost immediately overtaken by dreams of Latif trying to feed me candies from the ends of long tentacles.

It took far less time for me to be pulled from the dreams than I would have liked, but to my delight, it was Alex that woke me. Not some angry alphas determined to protect their omega's virtue from my *grabby* hands.

Before I could even sit up, he lumbered over to the bed, sinking gratefully down on the edge with a groan.

"What did you spend the day doing?" he asked.

"A few things," I said, trying to find my way out of the covers to sit up.

Alex was flushed red and sweating, looking like he was on the verge of passing out.

Frowning, I reached out, touching his forehead.

"What are you doing here?" I asked. "I thought you weren't feeling well."

He sighed.

"Yeah, I do feel like I'm about to crash again," he admitted. "But I felt bad leaving you on your own. We haven't even had time to go over all my work."

He winced, and I glanced down, eyes widening at the sight of his large belly shifting of its own accord.

"The little thing is getting impatient," he grumbled, setting a hand on top of the mound. "They're ready to get out."

I swallowed.

"Today?" I asked. "Because it kind of looks like it's about to happen."

"Don't think so," he said. "I'm pretty sure I'll have some warning first. Nothing's changed. Except that they seem impatient. Like there's not quite enough room anymore."

"That makes sense," I said. It didn't look like Alex could physically grow any bigger. For his sake, I hoped it wouldn't be much longer.

"Do you want to go over my work while I'm here?" he asked.

"I went through it all last night," I said. "It seems like you wanted to get into the history next, speak to the temple priest, and tour the caves."

"Yeah," he sighed. "It would be great if you could, but that doesn't seem very likely after the omega class you crashed."

I smiled.

"Well, I might have found a solution. Or stumbled into one, anyway."

"Oh?" he asked curiously, but before I could answer, an unwelcome voice rang through my new place.

"Alex?"

He grimaced.

"In here," he returned.

To my chagrin, Saar walked into my bedroom. He took one look at me and Alex, and a dark shadow crossed his face.

"Ah, here you are," he said coldly. "In Blaine's *bed*."

Before either of us could begin to argue, another alpha stepped out from behind Saar, entering the room.

"Well... welcome to the party," I said uneasily.

The alpha glared down at me, fury in his blood-orange gaze.

"So you're the human," he said in a low, gruff voice and I got the impression that whatever issue he had with me was personal.

"Let me guess," I said. "You're Latif's brother?"

His gaze narrowed further.

"So you do not deny personally knowing my brother," he growled. "An unmated omega."

I grimaced, but before I could speak, Alex pushed to his feet between us.

"It was my fault," he said. "I thought—"

"You do not yet know what he has done," Saar interrupted. "Allow your *friend* to explain."

All eyes turned to me.

Alex's were wide and filled with worry, and I wanted to ease that. At the same time, I wanted to smack Saar upside the head.

"I went to talk to the temple priest like you wanted me to." The alphas began to speak, but I raised my voice, talking over them while Alex's eyes widened comically. "Like we thought, I wasn't allowed in, but Latif happened to be there."

"And you convinced him to be your attendant!" the brother snapped.

"I—no." I sighed. "Hang on, at least let me get out of bed before you kick the shit out of me."

I got out of the covers and pushed to my own feet.

These two were big guys. Latif was small by comparison. But I held my ground, trying not to let it show.

"Priest Naz was the one to suggest it," I said firmly. "Me and Latif simply agreed."

All three of them gaped at me.

"It is not possible that you spoke to Priest Naz," the brother said, voice hushed. "No alpha is permitted to see the omega priest. And even if you did, why would he suggest such a thing?"

"I believe it had something to do with Latif not being allowed back at his classes," I suggested.

A dark shadow passed over his face.

"Latif has changed since beginning them. It is for his own good."

I nodded.

"Okay, well, I have no issue with that. It was just a trade. I'm not going to force anything."

For a moment, the large alpha didn't seem to know how to respond. He looked at Saar, seeming to be at a loss.

"Addy here came to give you trouble," Saar said.

"And you came to help," I supplied.

Saar pursed his lips.

"What you did *was* wrong. As a member of the council, it is my duty to settle these kinds of disputes."

"Right, and the fact that Alex is here with me has nothing to do with it," I muttered.

Anger flushed Saar's face.

"In one turn around the sun, you have already forgotten your place repeatedly," he snarled, taking a step forward. "You may be human, Blaine, but you are an alpha and you are not on Earth. You are here on Mukhana. That means you must abide by our laws."

"Got it," I snapped. "No mingling allowed."

"It is more than that," he argued. "Your flippant disregard will not be tolerated."

Anger that I had been trying to force down flooded me, filling me to the brim.

"My disregard?" I demanded. "What exactly did I do that is so wrong? Talk to an omega? On my first day here too. I get it. No more omegas. They need to be kept locked away like property."

"It is for their own protection!" Saar shouted, and a laugh burst from my lips.

"Typical toxic bullshit," I snapped. "When an omega gets stolen, do you consider it their fault too? You lot certainly don't take any accountability for your own actions."

Despite myself, I turned to Alex who was watching the exchange like the roof was falling.

"Is this really what you want?" I demanded incredulously. "What if your child is an omega? What then?"

He opened his mouth, wide eyes searching mine and, for a moment, he looked so overwhelmed that guilt replaced the fury blinding me—until Saar spoke for him.

"Alex is mine to work through things like that with. It is none of your concern."

He stepped forward, putting a possessive arm around Alex's shoulders and glaring down at me. If looks could kill, I would have been dead on the floor already. In fact, if I wasn't mistaken, the spikes on his back were standing higher, visible even from the front, like raised hackles.

"Take this as your warning, Blaine. If you make one more wrong move, I am personally calling your people to come retrieve you."

And with that, he turned, forcibly leading Alex from my bedroom.

"But we didn't go over my work yet," I heard Alex arguing as soon as they were out of sight. Saar's voice answered him quietly, but sternly, and my frustration only grew.

"And stay away from my brother," the other alpha—Addy, maybe?—snapped before turning and stalking from the room after them.

So, I guessed that meant Latif's parents had said no.

I groaned and collapsed into the chair at my desk, mind reeling.

Saar would just *love* to make the call to get me off this planet. What he didn't know, though, was that if I left, I would be taking Alex with me.

There had been something in his gaze when I'd said that, that told me I had hit home.

Alex didn't like the system here for the unmated omegas. He knew firsthand what happened to them; they got kidnapped and forced into a lifelong bond.

It had happened more than once already, and now

I was sure. Things had to change if any humans were to be left here.

What if the bonds began to go south? What if they faced abuse and imprisonment and per nassa customs, they had no way out. No one to turn to, no way to let the humans know, nowhere to run…

My gaze dropped to the files spread out in front of me.

I needed more evidence. I needed stories of bad things happening to omegas. I needed proof that it wasn't always good when they were mated.

Unless something drastic changed my mind, I needed to convince all of the humans to leave with me.

I swallowed, heart racing as the reality of what I wanted hit me properly.

And the fact that all the other omegas would remain here, stuck in this situation.

Latif's brash, strong personality would be stifled here.

I shut my eyes, wishing there was a way I could get to him, to tell him that he deserved so much more.

six

. . .

LATIF

Al-mother was *still* shouting when I stormed into my bedroom.

I half expected her to storm in here after me, and I didn't know what I would do. Perhaps physically push her out of my space or dive straight out the window. I could only imagine how she would react.

I swung around, looking at the large opening just as Addy strode into sight with a smug expression on his normally moody face.

He had gone to see Blaine. He had probably fought him and hurt him. Blaine was a gentle human. He didn't fight back. Not even against me.

Worry and frustration over the utter unfairness of the situation filled me to the point that my throat constricted.

Luckily my al-mother did not come after me. I could Om-father calming her down. Then the additional sound of Addy's voice arrived and told them whatever had happened with Blaine.

As I stood there, feeling utterly helpless and lost, my hands began to shake.

I had to leave here.

I would go to the temple. Naz would take me in if no one else would.

All because I had been born with the wrong pheromones.

I squeezed my eyes shut, allowing the traitorous thoughts to fill me. If only I had been an alpha. I would have freedom.

And completely take it for granted while turning a blind eye to the omegas in my life.

No. This was who I was meant to be.

An omega who could fight for myself and, somehow, change things for the rest of us.

I did not leave my room for the rest of the night. To my surprise, no one came in to check on me. Perhaps they were giving me space.

It wasn't until darkness had settled outside, and a chill filled the air that I heard someone approaching.

Sitting up in bed, I waited, watching as Om-father quietly entered.

I was impressed to see how he moved in near silence, clearly trying to keep the rest of the house from waking.

Sure enough, when he saw me sitting up, he pressed a finger to his lips, indicating that I shouldn't speak. Then, to my surprise, he gestured for me to follow him.

Heart rate spiking, I followed Om-father through the house, past the bedrooms, where Addy's and then Al-mother's breathing was loud and clear and undisturbed. Onto the quiet nighttime street, he led me.

I wrapped my arms around my cold shoulders and tried not to shiver.

"Where are we going?" I finally whispered, but he shushed me immediately.

Only once we had turned from the main street onto a quiet back alley, did he finally stop and turn to face me.

"Your mother," he began and, really, he needn't have said anything else, because I could hear the fury in his voice. "She would not even listen to me."

"She never listens," I said solemnly. "It's because we are omegas."

His gaze darkened.

"Please, Latif, stop saying things like that. I'm begging you."

I fell silent, waiting.

Om-father took a soft breath and released it, his shoulders sagging.

"Your mother is set in her ways, but she loves us and only wants what is best for us... but sometimes, she is rude. And we don't deserve that."

"So, what do you want to do?" I asked. "You still support her, yet brought me all the way out here. For what?"

"For you," he said tiredly. "You are my child, Latif. I would do anything for you. Even face your mother's wrath."

"Does that mean—?"

"It means that I will arrange everything. If Blaine still agrees."

I stared as my om-father began to walk again. It took me a moment to hurry and fall into step at his side.

"What do you mean?" I asked, hope filling me.

"It means you do as we agreed earlier today. You show Blaine around, and you go to auction and in exchange, you get your classes back."

My steps faltered.

"After I am mated, you mean?"

"Will you do it otherwise?"

"Of course!" I lied.

He paused and met my eyes.

After a moment, he shook his head.

"It will only be a few days. You can wait. Do not tell your Al-mother," he said sternly. I nodded, hope filling me as we slowed at the back of a house I didn't recognize.

Om-father stepped up to one of the windows.

"Hello?" he whispered. "Blaine? Are you there?"

There was a sudden shuffling and the sound of something falling, then stillness.

After a long moment, the human man appeared in the dark window, hanging back as though he was worried.

It seemed to take a moment for him to recognize us. When he did, he let out a relieved sigh.

"You again," he said, his cloudy gaze meeting mine. "I don't think either of you should be here or I'm going to be dealing with your alphas in the morning."

My stomach twisted, but I realized he looked tired, but otherwise fine. Relief filled me as I realized that they hadn't hurt him.

"I apologize for my Addy," Om-father said, "but I am here to make a deal with you."

"I'm not sure I want to ask," Blaine said, but Om-father went on as though he hadn't spoken.

"If you stick to the arrangement we made today, Latif will be your guide."

He stared, fist at Om-father, then at me.

"Why would you even *want* that?" he asked.

"Latif does not listen to me," Om-father said, "but I believe he will listen to you."

"About the auctions?" he asked hesitantly.

Om-father nodded.

I watched the exchange silently.

The fact that he thought I would not listen to him, that I would only listen to an alpha, hurt.

Perhaps he did not understand me at all. Perhaps none of them did.

It took a moment for me to realize they were both watching me, waiting for my input.

I swallowed and nodded, avoiding looking at Blaine and the way his eyes seemed to see straight into me.

"How much do you need from him?" Om-father asked.

"Uh—I need to see the caves. Talk about the temple since I can't go in there. Go over the societal structure—"

"Four meetings," Om-father said firmly. "Is that enough?"

Blaine nodded.

"Yes, okay. Deal," he said breathlessly.

Om-father took inhaled softly, steeling himself for a moment as though he was suddenly unsure.

"Go back to the temple after the first morning light. Latif will be there."

Blaine met my gaze and gave a rueful grin.

"I'm ready if you are."

I nodded resolutely but remained silent and stayed that way as we returned down dark alleys to our home.

Our breaths hitched as we entered, listening to hear if the others had noticed our absence, but the house remained quiet.

Just before entering his room, Om-father placed a hand on my arm, stopping me.

"This is for your happiness," Om-father whispered. "Don't make me regret it."

I managed a nod, but what little chance I had of sleeping after that was obliterated.

Energy tingled through my entire nervous system.

At dawn I would be taken to the temple. Blaine would come to retrieve me. What would Naz say? Surely, expecting the priest to lie for us was too much.

Why had Om-father done this? Was it really that important to him for me to bond with an alpha?

A thought niggled in my brain that perhaps there

was something more to bonding. Something only those who were bonded could truly know…

Racing thoughts carried me nearly all the way to dawn and even then, when I slept it was short lived.

I woke up, tense and tired, just as the sky began to lighten.

Addy strolled into my room not long after that. Seeing me dressed and reading a book, he paused, mid-yawn, to stare at me.

"Goddess, you look terrible."

"Watch your language," I said.

"Why?" he asked. "You're suddenly religious?"

I glared.

"I *do* work at the temple weekly," I reminded him.

Addy smirked.

"You're about to be there a lot more than that."

I stilled.

He already knew. Om-father had told them the lie…

"Oh?" I found myself asking.

"As punishment," Addy said, taking pleasure in delivering the news. "And to try to *get you back on the right path,* according to Om-father."

I swallowed, gazing at the floor in hopes that he wouldn't be able to read my expression. I shouldn't have been concerned. Addy wasn't perceptive enough for noticing the subtle emotions of others.

"When will this punishment begin?" I asked.

"Right now," he said, grinning. "I'm going to deliver you."

He was enjoying this *far* too much. I didn't want to let him. I wanted to fall into our usual roles of bickering siblings, but this one time, I couldn't make too much of a fuss. Just in case Al-mother got involved.

Instead, I pushed to my feet, giving him nothing but a glare that only made his smile larger.

It appeared that Om-father was a spectacular actor, because he handed me a breakfast pack, wrapped in a cloth, as we entered the main room. He appeared worried but sympathetic with no trace of our scheme visible on his face.

"It will only be for a short while," he reassured.

"We hope you learn from this," Al-mother added from the corner, where she was lounging, still looking half asleep.

I gritted my teeth, turning to Addy.

"Lead the way," I said, gesturing to the door.

He did so with a bounce in his step, and the reason was clear as soon as we were on the street.

"You know, you brought this on yourself. You've been way out of line with a lot of things lately.

Great, I was going to be lectured the entire way.

I let him ramble on as we walked. This early in

the morning, the streets were empty and the air too cold.

As we reached the path to the temple, which was just within the skirt of the jungle, his words were finally too much for me.

"You act out too much," he was saying. "You just don't know how to play along."

"What do you know about playing along?" I demanded. "They don't make you do *anything* you don't want to."

"You're an *omega*," he reminded me, straining the word in an altogether obnoxious way. "It seems like you keep forgetting that fact. You should try to be a bit more like Alil."

"Alil?!" I spluttered. "What do you know about Alil? You've barely even *seen* him."

He shrugged sheepishly.

"I don't need to see him more than I have to know that he is a good omega. He always looks away when I'm near."

"Yes, and then runs and hides because you are an *unmated alpha*. In case *you* have forgotten. We have been taught to fear you."

His jaw clenched, gaze fixing forward angrily, and thank the goddess, from that moment on he remained blissfully silent until we reached the entrance to the jungle.

Anywhere else was more or less out of bounds, but the temple path was walled off on all sides. After all, it was meant to be a safe haven for omegas.

"I can go the rest of the way alone," I said, and he nodded dismissively.

It wasn't exactly forbidden, but it was frowned upon for any alphas to come closer than this. Hence why the three to arrive yesterday had been such a shock.

"Om-father will come collect you later."

"When?" I asked, but Addy was already stalking away.

Strange.

Why would he care so much that Alil would be afraid of him? Unless he wanted him...

My stomach dropped at the sudden thought.

Alil was my age. We had both waited too long to mate. It wasn't out of the question that my brother would fight for him. For some reason, the thought of it, my best friend and my brother becoming close, bothered me.

I shook the thought away.

Even if I was right, what were the chances that Addy would win him?

I reached the temple just as the sun lifted past the horizon. Instead of entering, I took a seat on one of the steps and allowed the sounds of the jungle to occupy me.

It was interesting that the temple had been placed somewhere so dangerous. Perhaps the alphas needed a serious deterrent, even if the danger wasn't real. Not anymore anyway.

When it had first been built over four hundred years ago, the jungle had not been blocked off. The omegas must have been desperate to have their own space. Maybe that was something I could tell Blaine.

"Latif?"

I glanced back at the sound of Naz's surprised voice from behind me.

He was standing at the top step, hugging a robe around his shoulders to protect himself against the morning chill.

"What are you doing here so early?" he asked. "Did you need to clear your head? Or—oh."

He fell silent, gaze fixed on the new arrival.

I grimaced as I realized that Blaine was already striding the last few steps toward the temple.

"So, I assume your parents ended up agreeing to the plan?" Naz asked.

I shrugged sheepishly.

"Well, one of them did."

Naz frowned. "I see..."

"Good morning," Blaine called up.

Naz gave him a weak wave.

"Seeing an alpha twice in so many days after years apart from them isn't good for my heart," he said. "I'm going back inside. Just know that, even though I support you making your own choice, I won't lie about it either."

"I doubt Al-mother is going to be coming here asking questions," I reassured.

Naz nodded, still looking dubious as he disappeared back within the temple.

I pushed slowly to my feet, descending to meet Blaine.

Just like our first meeting in the field, a defensiveness filled me. My body grew tenser the closer I came, and finally, I realized that this was our first time alone together.

"Ready?" he asked.

I nodded breathlessly as his pheromones enveloped me.

A shiver ran through my body.

"We have to keep a low profile," he said as we began to walk. "Have any suggestions for things we can do without being seen?"

"You said you wanted to explore the caves," I said, keeping my voice carefully neutral. "They aren't guarded."

"Lead the way," he said.

I nodded, turning in the direction of the mountains as we left the jungle. The entrance to the caves were not all the way in foothills, but in the rocky ground that led there.

It was a long walk. And so early, when everything was so quiet, the silence between us was deafening.

"Why do you even want to do this?" I found myself asking, just to end the quiet.

"Just to help Alex out," Blaine said. "We've been friends for a long time, and I owe him a couple favors."

"Were you friends on the human planet?" I asked.

Blaine shook his head.

"No, actually. We didn't know each other until Alex joined my HFC crew about five years ago."

"HFC?"

"Human First Contact," he explained patiently. "We reach out to new planets and try to establish alliances."

I nodded as though I understood, but I could not even imagine the type of life they must have led before coming here.

"What about you?" he asked carefully. "I'm guessing that this is your first time out on your own?"

The way he looked at me, with his sharp gray

gaze peering through me, searching for something, set me on edge.

"No, actually," I argued. "I go to the bathhouse with my friends, and I go to classes."

"Jiujitsu," he said, wincing. "Don't remind me."

"Not just that. I have done various training since I was a child. Music. Reading. Writing. Various art forms. And cooking."

For a while, he did not respond.

My gaze kept flying to his profile, wondering what he was thinking.

Why did I get the impression that he wasn't happy with my arguments?

"So you like being an omega?" he suddenly asked. "You like needing to be escorted places and having to stay behind walls and being considered property?"

The disdain was clear in his tone, but his words shocked me. For a moment I did not know what to say, and my feet stopped moving of their own accord.

After continuing for a few steps without me, Blaine paused and turned back around to face me.

"I've never heard anyone say it like that but me."

He stared, understanding filling his gaze, and, to my surprise, a smile lifted his lips.

"Well, Latif," he said gently, "let me tell you what a pleasant surprise this is."

seven

. . .

BLAINE

It was like the floodgates had been opened. Once my stance had been made clear, Latif couldn't stop talking about it and the more he did, the more my base concerns were confirmed.

"It's ridiculous that we cannot attend any celebrations," he was ranting. "We would be safe in such large crowds, surely."

"You absolutely would," I agreed. "I can't imagine you allowing someone to touch you without your consent."

He glanced at me through his dark blue lashes, almost shyly, and chuckled.

"You know, you are supposed to be convincing me to enter the auctions," he reprimanded gently, and I found myself smiling playfully.

"I believe I said I would *talk* to you about the auctions. I don't think what I would say was addressed at all."

He bit his lip, leading me over the rocky path that didn't look like a path at all.

"So… what is your opinion of them?" he asked hesitantly.

Maybe he thought that I would suddenly change my stance now that the topic was at hand, because he was tense again, shooting me worried glances.

"I…" How to say it gently?

He stopped walking and waited for me to finish the thought.

Pausing, my gaze fell over Latif's lithe form, despite myself.

He was like a willow tree, slender and gentle. Even the way he moved was soft but filled with grounded strength.

"You're beautiful," I said honestly. "And its nature for many cultures to try to collect and own beautiful things. But possession is not love and you may be beautiful, but you are also strong-willed and resilient."

"Why are you saying this?" Latif asked, his voice uncertain.

I shrugged helplessly.

"Because you are able to make your own choices. And that should mean more than winning a fight to your alphas."

"As in… I should bond, but only to someone I choose myself?"

"If you *want* to. Yes."

"If not, then they should respect that."

I sighed, suddenly hearing myself.

"I shouldn't be saying any of this," I admitted. "I'm pushing my own ideals onto you."

I couldn't help but be a little disgusted with myself, but Latif's next words soothed me.

"No," he said firmly. "We share our ideals… and you are the first person that I have ever heard speaking the way that I think."

He bit his lip, and a small fang dug into the flesh.

"It's… empowering," he whispered.

Satisfaction filled me.

I wasn't sure what else to call it. Maybe pride too. I had been right to question things. Where there was smoke, there was always fire. How many other omegas felt trapped with no support?

"Come," he said. "We are almost there."

I allowed him to take me the rest of the way until we stopped on a small ledge.

"You may enter first," he said.

Pausing, I glanced around, seeing nothing but rock around us. The sun was up high now, the hint of the second sun poking over the horizon, promising to make the day even hotter. But even under the bright light of the day, no cave mouth caught my eye.

"Sorry, where?" I asked.

"Just there," Latif said, gesturing to the ground.

I followed his gaze and balked at the sight of the small hole in the ground. It was approximately two feet in width, and far less in height.

"Please don't tell me *that* is the entrance to the legendary omega caves."

Latif chuckled.

"It widens out once you are within the tunnels."

I grimaced and looked around.

We'd been walking for about two hours now and I didn't fancy going to all this trouble just to head back empty-handed. Not to mention Latif needed me to get back to doing what he loved.

In the distance, the city looked calm and quiet, so at least there was plenty of time for Latif to pull me back out if I got stuck.

"Me first?" I asked, hoping Latif would argue that, but he only nodded.

Sighing, I dropped to my knees and shuffled as close to the hole as I could to peer inside.

It didn't look like a direct drop. The ground was a slanted sheet of hard rock for the two feet I could see.

Bracing myself, I pushed through the threshold.

As expected, it was a tight fit. The rock touched me on each side if I shifted the wrong way but offered just enough space to squeeze through.

Far too soon, darkness enveloped me, adding to the claustrophobic feeling.

Behind me, what little light there was, was suddenly blotted out by Latif's body, sliding in after me.

"Shit," I muttered, feeling around aimlessly. "Don't suppose you brought a flashlight, or candle, or something?"

I reached forward and suddenly realized there was room for my arms to spread out. No walls on each side. Tentatively, I reached above and to my immense relief, realized that I had come out of the passage into a larger space.

Heart thumping, I sat up, sliding out of the way for Latif to enter.

He sat up, panting softly at my side.

"There are torches in the caverns," he said. "But the light from the entrance is enough for right here."

"Is it?" I asked, looking around blindly.

Aside from the dim light at the end of the tunnel we'd just crawled through, I saw nothing at all.

Suddenly, Latif's soft fingers touched my chin, tilting my face toward him.

"Oh," he said softly. "You can't see me, can you?"

I shook my head.

"No. Can you see me?"

"Yes," he breathed, and it was that moment that I realized he hadn't released my chin yet. Instead, very tentatively, his fingertips brushed over the stubble there.

My heart was already racing from being in here. Suddenly the speed amplified.

I reached up, but the moment my hand touched his, he gasped and pulled away.

I could only guess where exactly he was, but I reached out and my hand found his arm.

"It's okay," I said gently. "I know you're not used to being around alphas."

I heard him swallow.

"Good thing we can't get into any trouble without being bonded, right?"

My breath hitched at the thought. Latif *was* very attractive. There was no denying that.

"Right." Latif finally whispered, but there was something in his voice that rang through me.

"Am I wrong?" I asked.

His silence was my answer. Surprise reverberated through me.

"But—the alphas in the bathhouse. They said that nassa aren't able to have intercourse until they've been bonded."

"The alphas don't know," Latif said in a quiet voice. "Oh Goddess, I shouldn't be telling you this."

"Wow," I breathed. "So the alphas have no idea."

"Om-father took me aside when I reached that age and explained everything to me and taught me how to control my desires."

"Control them?"

"Yes. With exercise and the temple."

I blinked.

"And the alphas…?"

"They get a taste of it during puberty but then it stops until they are bonded. It's nature's way of making them want a bond, you see."

I couldn't quite believe my ears.

Suddenly, I laughed.

"I don't know why I find this so funny," I chuckled. "I know I shouldn't, it's just these alphas act so macho and virile."

"It isn't funny!" Latif snapped. "Do you know how hard it is to suppress these urges?"

I shook my head.

"Why suppress them though?" I asked.

Silence met my question.

"You already rebel against everything else," I mused. "Why choose to deny the one thing that will actually make you feel good?"

Again, Latif was silent.

"I—I never thought of it like that before," he finally said.

I won't corrupt the innocent omega, I told myself.

Then again…

"Who are you saving yourself for?" I asked. "Your future alpha mate?"

I felt Latif shudder next to me.

"I suppose not," he muttered.

We lapsed into a tense silence. I almost wanted to reach out again, to find him in the dark and—then what?

If I so much as touched a hair on his head, Saar and Addy, and every other alpha on this planet, would probably kill me. That polite call for a pickup would be gone, replaced by a "missing" persons report.

"It will be difficult for you to get to the caverns if you cannot see," Latif said, suddenly changing the subject. "You may hold my arm if you like."

I nodded.

"Sure," I breathed, disappointed despite myself.

There was the sound of shuffling and a moment

later, Latif pulled my arm, making me realize I should stand.

I hadn't expected there to be standing room here, and there *wasn't*. I found out, by banging my head against the rocks above us.

"Sorry," Latif hissed. "I should have told you the ceiling is low."

I shook my head, rubbing the spot.

"All good," I said, turning toward his voice.

I reached out, finding his arm at once and then letting my hand slide down to grip his.

"Lead the way."

Latif didn't move.

I strained in the darkness to see him even though it was pointless.

"You're aroused," Latif suddenly whispered.

I grimaced.

I hadn't thought of the fact that if he could see me relatively clearly, he would see the way my cock was stretching my pants.

"Uh. Yeah," I agreed. "I guess our conversation got to me."

I chuckled awkwardly, but Latif's grip on my hand tightened.

"I am too," he murmured.

My mouth went dry. Despite myself, I tried to see in the darkness, but I didn't need to.

"Feel," Latif breathed and suddenly pressed the back of my hand to his length.

I inhaled sharply, but before anything else could be done, I was shoved roughly away.

Unable to see in the dark, I stumbled before the rough cave wall caught me.

"I should go back," Latif gasped.

I heard the sound of his frantic breathing as he bent and began to crawl back the way we had come.

For a moment, I stood in the darkness, stunned.

I hadn't expected such a response. After all, he had made me touch him. The feeling of his hard cock under silky fabric still burned the back of my hand.

Swallowing, I bent to follow him.

Even after such a short time within the cave, the sun burned my eyes.

It took me a moment to see where Latif was, sitting on a stone slab, anxiously chewing a nail. He stared into the distance, toward the city, frowning.

Grimacing, I came to his side and slowly lowered myself next to him.

"It seems like everyone else is right," Latif whispered.

"About what?" I asked. "Don't tell me you mean about alphas and omegas mingling."

"I can barely stand to be next to you for too long," he whispered. "You're enticing."

Although a wave of pleasure flooded my body at his words, I shook my head.

"You're stronger than that," I informed him. "You've never been around an unmated alpha for long, right? Maybe you just need some practice."

He smiled wryly.

"Are you saying we should keep trying, even though I instigated something inappropriate with you?"

"Why not?" I asked.

"Hm. I wonder what you would get from such an arrangement?" he said, rolling his eyes.

I arched a brow.

"Who says I would let you?"

Startled, he looked at me. For a moment I was struck by the color of his eyes. In the light of the sun, they reminded me of something. It took me a moment to remember the glass suncatcher that had mesmerized me in the market. Latif's eyes were just the same.

"You mean to tell me, you would stop me?" he asked, sounding dumbfounded, and then hesitantly, he added, "Am I not attractive to you?"

I swallowed.

"Oh, no," I breathed. "I am *definitely* not saying that."

He bit his lip, turning his gaze away again.

"If you don't want to get intimate with me, I'll just stop you if you try," I said. "Easy as that."

"But... we both..."

"Got hard?" I supplied. "That doesn't mean we need to act on it, Latif."

He took a shaky breath.

"If—" he swallowed. "If you can say no, then perhaps I can use you as practice. I need to prove I can be around unmated alphas when the time comes."

"What are you planning?" I asked, curious.

This time, when his gaze met mine, it was filled with strength and determination.

"I don't know yet," he said. "But I will not remain behind a wall for much longer."

I didn't doubt it.

And I didn't think I had ever been so impressed with someone.

"You have no idea, Latif," I said, just as sure. "I'll be your biggest supporter."

eight

. . .

LATIF

I felt like I was going to be sick when I saw Addy marching down the path to retrieve me. I was sure he would be able to tell that something had happened, but apparently, he wasn't in the mood to pay me any attention. In fact, he barely looked at me as we walked back home.

Honestly, it was a relief.

I didn't trust my acting abilities. I didn't even trust my mouth to not immediately blurt out something that it shouldn't. It wasn't entirely my fault, either. How was I supposed to stop thinking of the fact that I had made someone touch me like that?

What had come over me? Was it just pheromones? Were they truly that strong?

Warnings I'd heard all my life about staying apart until I was mated rang through my ears at deafening volume. Blaine's parting words were just as loud, that "attraction is natural, but remember you don't have to act on it."

His words were comforting though. They made perfect sense, too. I had never been around unmated alphas. I didn't yet know how to control myself in their presence. That was all. I needed practice. I needed more time with Blaine. Just the two of us.

The thought made heat rush through my body and my stomach drop.

I forced my mind clear as we entered the house.

Al-mother was already back from the river. She looked tired, as she often did after a day spent on the boat, wrestling fish from the water. But normally, on her workdays, she was gone until long after sundown.

"Al-mother," I said, surprised, "why are you here?"

"Your Al-mother hurt herself," Om-father chastised, emerging from the kitchen with a bowl of water, ointment, and wrapping cloths.

I realized Al-mother had her foot up on a pillow.

It looked swollen and two of the claws were snapped off near the base.

I winced, but she only shrugged.

"Just a minor slip, but they sent me home since I wasn't steady on my feet after that."

I nodded and went to sit next to her. Even though I was still annoyed with her, I couldn't stop myself from getting involved, and began to help Om-father by spreading the ointment onto the broken edges while he did the bruised ankle.

Addy watched for a moment and then huffed and marched away.

"What's wrong with him?" Al-mother asked. "Did you say something to him? He's been in a sour mood since this morning."

I pursed my lips.

"Well, let me just say that if Alil ever goes to auction, Addy will be the first in line to fight."

"Alil?" Om-father asked with interest, a warm smile blooming on his pretty face. "That would be a lovely match, wouldn't it? And your best friend would be part of the family."

I grunted in response, not wanting to comment. The idea of Alil getting bonded still made me feel like I was being left behind. We'd been glued to each other's sides for so many years.

"And what do you mean *if* he goes to auction?"

Al-mother chimed in. "Not all omegas are like you, Latif. They actually want to find mates and be happy."

"What makes you think I won't be happy without an alpha?" I asked through gritted teeth.

"Not this again," Om-father sighed, cutting in. "You've had a long day, Latif. Go to your room. Your Al-mother needs to rest, not argue."

I gave him a look, annoyed despite the lengths he was going to for me.

"And what about my classes?" I demanded instead of listening. "I'm doing punishment and working at the temple. When will I be allowed to go back?"

"Latif," Al-mother began, her voice stern, but Om-father cut in once more.

"If you behave," he warned, "you may be able to go again. But for now, you can stay home or go to the temple."

"Whatever you say," I sighed.

Om-father was soaking the wraps in the bowl of water, so I set the ointment down on the floor and pushed to my feet.

"I will be in my room rereading old books, I suppose, for the rest of the evening."

As I reached the hallway, I heard Al-mother's voice murmuring something.

"He is not happy with us right now," Om-father responded. "He needs some space."

That was an understatement.

I wanted out of this house.

I did not know where I would go or what my life would look like if I did, but something needed to change. I needed to experience life and not just the one that they deemed fit for me. I was glad that Om-father at least seemed to understand that a little bit... even if his end goal was only for me to be handed over for someone else to control. Honestly, better my own mother than another alpha that I didn't know. That was part of why none of this made sense for me.

I pulled the heavy curtain shut between us and stood for a moment, looking around my room. It was filled with things to occupy me. There was a large bookshelf on the wall, filled with books I had already read. An easel was placed carefully in front of the window. Before, when I'd been fixated on painting, that simple view had been replicated more than once by my skilled hands. There were countless scrolls of different sunsets piled beneath my bed.

A desk held papers and pens and various trinkets, some of which remained from my trinket-making days. For a while, I had been obsessed with making little wired critters that were fully posable. I still liked them and sometimes fidgeted with them, but they were a sign to me of my boredom now.

I imagined that all omegas had rooms like this. Filled with the outcomes of years of keeping oneself busy.

Now, seeing it all, just made me feel sad and sorry for myself... The old me, anyway. The one who had nothing to look forward to.

Devin had already changed me, but now, after one day spent with Blaine, I felt different.

The way he spoke to me made me feel respected. He made me feel like I was right to want all the things I wanted.

Even when I had done something wrong, he didn't act like I had. Instead, he had spoken about why I had done it and how to move past that.

And the fact that he was an alpha did make it even better. He had no reason to want my freedom for me, yet he did.

Perhaps it was a human way of thinking, but I didn't think so. He was not the first human I'd gotten to know.

Blaine was different.

He was special.

And yes, he smelled like every sinfully good thing in the world rolled into one delicious human body.

I shivered, remembering how close we had gotten, how without the flow of air in that cave his scent had enveloped me.

And his body. Oh, Goddess forgive me, but the sight of his erection was burned into my eyelids. I could not imagine wanting to feel anything else in the world so much.

I swallowed, squeezing my eyes shut in an attempt at pushing it all away again.

Now that I was alone in my room though, it was futile.

Blaine's words rang in my ears.

"Why choose to deny the one thing that will actually make you feel good?"

"Oh," I breathed. Goddess, he was so right. Why did I always fight these urges when they could offer me relief?

Hands trembling, I reached down, gripping the edges of my robe.

I never did this. I had before I'd built up the willpower to stop myself, but it had been so long...

It felt obscene to pull my clothes off and simply see the state I was in. My length was hard, and desperate to be touched, dampness was building in my hole, my body felt hot and itchy deep inside.

Normally, this was when I exercised breathing and meditating and if that did not help, I would exercise. The last thing I would do was act on it. Even looking crossed the line. Yet now that I did, I could not ignore the reality that I was a sexual being, one that wanted to feel that part of life too.

Slowly, I reached down, brushing my fingers over the tip.

Even the small touch made pleasure shudder through my body.

Shaking, I gripped my length, gaze flying to the doorway. Any moment now, Om-father could come check on me. He never announced his arrival. At least as alphas, the other two were more careful.

Still, the thought made me panic. Not enough to stop, but enough to back toward the furthest corner and lean against it.

If he entered, I would have a second to drop my robes before he saw me. That would have to do, because I couldn't stop. I stroked my length frantically, eager to finish as quickly as possible and it didn't take me long because I looked down and suddenly, I saw Blaine's strong hand, his beige skin, the fine hairs on the back of his arm.

A guttural moan tore from my throat before I bit my lips hard, trying to stop the sound that wanted to come out of me as my body clenched. Liquid spurted from my tip, enough to slick my length while my hole clenched, desperate to be touched, slick dripping between my thighs.

My legs were shaking so hard, I slipped down the wall, sitting in a slump where I had been standing, frantically pulling the fabric of my robe back down to shield myself from view.

Heart still racing, I listened as hard as I could for any sign that I had been heard. After a moment, I realized I could hear the other three talking from the main room and sighed in relief.

I had to clean myself up and go back to pretending that none of today had happened. But I couldn't do it quite yet.

I felt weak and suddenly overwhelmed because doing what I had just done hadn't offered the relief I had been seeking.

Blaine was right that it was my body, that I should do what I pleased with it.

And now, I wanted more.

nine

. . .

BLAINE

Latif was already walking up the path toward me when I neared the temple the next day. We hadn't even set a proper time to meet so I was glad to see him, but the sentiment did not appear to be returned.

He barely even looked at me as we walked and only offered a nod in greeting, expecting me to fall into step next to him, which I did.

The previous day he had been so excited to talk to me, to express all his opinions and ideals. Maybe he was feeling shy after what had happened. I certainly hadn't been able to stop thinking about it. The earnest way he had shown me his arousal had kept me up half the night.

I shot him glances the whole time we walked, but he stoically kept his eyes facing forward or looking at the ground. That gave me plenty of time to look at him. His long black hair was tied tightly on top of his head. He wasn't in anything glittery today. His small shoulder bag was his only accessory, but his tunic was pretty, as usual, in a deep teal color that looked silky to the touch and flowed with his movements.

He must have felt my appreciative gaze, because finally, he bit his lip, glanced in my direction, and then quickly looked the other way.

"Latif," I finally said, "are you planning on ignoring me for the entire day?"

"What? No—I'm not," he spluttered, finally turning and facing me. And then he stood staring at me for a moment, his chest heaving. His gaze traveled down my body before he spun back around, hiding his face with his hands.

For a moment, I stood there, a bit dumbfounded and then flattered, despite myself. These nassa men were attractive beyond the level of a normal human man like me. Yet I was the one that Latif was looking at like that.

I had to close my eyes for a moment and bite back

the pleasure that filled me and hurried to catch up to Latif.

"It's only pheromones," I said, and he jumped like I had yelled.

"I can't talk about this right now," he said, sounding flustered.

"Why?" I asked, looking around.

We'd taken the same route as yesterday toward the cave and there was no one anywhere near. The city was miles away.

Latif followed my gaze and sagged a little bit.

"I don't trust myself," he finally admitted in a quiet voice.

"Don't trust yourself?" I repeated.

"Please," he said, suddenly meeting my eyes again. "Wait until we are in the cave."

I was powerless to say no to him, so remained silent and curious until we reached the spot again.

This time, knowing where to look, I saw the cave entrance as we neared.

"After you," I said, gesturing for him to go first.

Latif took a breath and nodded, still looking tense and nervous when our eyes met.

Surprised, I watched him hoist his robe up and then get down on his knees. I really shouldn't have been watching as he crawled into the narrow opening, but I couldn't help myself.

I'd nearly forgotten about the tail though, and that seemed to hide most of the view I was unconsciously looking for.

Still, to be polite, I waited a minute before following. The poor guy was already nervous enough after yesterday.

Pushing the thought away, I pulled the small utility tool from my pocket, flipped it open, and turned on the flashlight before entering after him.

It still felt incredibly claustrophobic, even with the light on and when I emerged on the other side, Latif was shielding his eyes.

"What is that?" he demanded.

I pointed it away hastily.

"It's just a flashlight," I said. "To help me see."

"I guess this was pointless then," he said, pulling a small candle from his bag.

He was still squinting though, so I flicked the flashlight off and tucked it away.

"The candle will be a bit gentler on the eyes, actually," I said.

He didn't reply, but after a moment, a light flickered on.

For a moment, we watched each other. Then I remembered why we were supposed to be here and looked around for the first time.

The cave we were sitting in was small and bare

and only a few feet wide, but there were two passages off of it.

"Does no one else ever enter this place?" I asked.

"Only rarely," Latif said. "We used to come here on class trips sometimes. My classmates and I would run around the tunnels playing games."

That explained a lot. I couldn't imagine this being used as frequently as the other omega spots, like the temple, but the idea of children disregarding the history to play games made me smile. It seemed they were the same anywhere you went.

"Come this way," he said, gesturing for me to follow him.

He led me to one of the passages, which led to a long, steep staircase that I was so glad we hadn't attempted when I couldn't see a thing. I clung to the thin metal railing like my life depended on it as we descended. That was when things got interesting.

It took me a few minutes before I realized that there were carvings in the walls and the further down we went, the more detailed they became.

As we emerged into a cavernous room, I was breathless with wonder.

"What is this place?" I asked quietly.

"This is where the ancient omegas came to write their stories," Latif explained. At the look of wonder on my face, he added, "Why did you think these were called the omega caves?"

I shook my head, slowly turning in a circle to see all angles of the room.

"Do you mind if I turn my flashlight back on?" I asked.

Latif shook his head, smiling softly as he watched me.

"It is amazing, isn't it?" he asked.

As I turned on my flashlight and the room was flooded with light, I couldn't agree more. I had seen many things in my lifetime, but to be exposed first-hand to something from ancient history that was preserved so well was moving.

The carvings were far from the simple cave drawings of ancient Earth. They were clearly from a later stage of evolution. They were intricate and detailed. Nassa faces so real, they must have been based on living people, looked down at us. Around them, landscapes and designs filled the space, mountains, waterfalls, and wilderness. Far above us, a grand figure looked down, her arms open as though welcoming us.

"The goddess," Latif said, following my gaze. "And the story of our creation."

He pointed up, directing my gaze.

"See there," he said, and I realized there was a

flow to the carvings. They went around the room in a spiral if you followed it properly. But each of the goddess's hands seemed to be a different starting point.

"This is a story?" I asked, and I thought I could see it.

The Goddess created two parts: an alpha and an omega. From each hand, a different sequence of events began.

"The alphas were given the gift of strength," Latif said. "They dealt with difficulties. They faced the wilderness and learned how to survive it. They became warriors."

I followed the images as Latif explained and realized that the alpha in the carvings were first shown fighting giant animals, things that looked like snakes and alligators and giant birds. Then they stood victorious.

On the other side, in tandem, the omegas seemed to be connecting to the stars. Their eyes were closed, minds linked to the wilderness around them.

"The omegas learned the connection between life and the universe," Latif went on. "And how to bring alphas to balance."

Mesmerized, I realized that the stories converged to couples in intimate poses, foreheads pressed together, or limbs tangled in Kamasutra-like positions.

As it reached the last level, there were countless different figures, many holding children. In each, the omegas were surrounded by flowers.

"What does this mean?" I asked, indicating the crowd of figures and flowers.

He crossed his arms, hugging himself as though he was cold.

"It means that we omegas were given the gift of creating life. That we hold the power of growth and love."

A shiver traveled over me.

I had been expecting to learn negative things about the lives of omegas here on Mukhana. Instead, I was faced with a beautiful thought.

The omegas *were* the ones with all the power here. After all, alphas could not even become aroused without them.

Their historic cave painted them at peace with the alphas and each other. Free and loving and happy.

Then again, Latif was given no autonomy whatsoever. None of them were.

When had things gone so wrong?

Suddenly, I found myself watching Latif instead of the walls. He gazed up at the story, his eyes traveling over it almost sadly. Here Latif was, a living, breathing connection to this story and he was far more captivating.

"Didn't you want to talk to me?" I asked, drawing him from whatever thoughts were making him frown so much.

His eyes flew to mine. They were black in this lighting. As was his hair. It was so easy to look at him as a lost young man who carried too much on his shoulders.

As we looked at each other, an overwhelming urge came over me. I wanted to help him somehow. In any way I could.

I wanted him to be happy. Because he didn't seem to be right now. No, he seemed to be tense and conflicted and filled with anger.

If only I could soothe those feelings for him.

He swallowed.

"I don't want to talk in front of them," he whispered.

I glanced around and a chill traveled over me.

"Do you think they're listening?"

He shook his head, but his expression said otherwise.

"It feels like they are, doesn't it?"

I looked around at all the stone eyes, so many of them turned down toward us that I shivered.

"Yes," I agreed. "Let's go back."

"This way," Latif said, picking up his candle and gesturing to another passageway.

I followed him, flicking my flashlight off as we entered.

I could see images in the flickering of the candle-light but didn't ask about them. This cave held a wealth of information and secrets about the nassa. I could probably study it for years. How unfortunate that I didn't see myself, or any other human, being here for much longer.

A large staircase rose before us, but Latif directed me another way, through a narrow passage, toward the sound of running water, and into a small cavern.

Water poured from a fissure above, into a small pool. It was filled with tile work so intricate that I was blown away once more. Every surface in the room was part of a larger flower design and all the different colored stones seemed to shimmer. Then I caught sight of something glowing in the depths of the water and approached slowly.

I watched the little glowing fish, swimming peacefully under the water. Behind me, I heard Latif blow out the candle so I could see it better. I stood there mesmerized, until I felt Latif come up behind me.

The brush of his robes on the backs of my legs made me shiver and when I turned around, he was standing closer than he should have been, only inches between us and a look in his eyes that said he wanted to close even that distance.

My stomach swooped, yesterday's conversation flying back to mind.

"Latif," I said, soft but firm. "Remember what we said. It's just the pheromones. We don't have to act on this."

He bowed his head, thick lashes fluttering as he lowered his gaze.

"It's not just the pheromones," he whispered. "I won't be having an auction, Blaine. I won't ever have an alpha to mate with."

He swallowed and reached out, touching my arm with a shaking hand.

"We have three days left. This is my only chance."

My heart raced at his words. How could I possibly deny him now? He was right.

Without thinking about it anymore, I stepped up to him, winding my other arm around his waist.

I wasn't one to rock the boat, but if Latif wanted to rebel with *me*, then I wasn't going to tell him *no*, either. I wanted him. To show him how good he could feel, to rock his world. Even to give him good memories, because, yeah, he was right. This was probably the only time he was ever going to feel someone touching him, making love to him, without expecting anything in return.

I pulled him in tightly, crushing our bodies together, feeling the hard length of his cock against mine as it swiftly joined the party.

A ragged gasp tore from his throat, and he seemed to collapse against me, wrapping both arms around my shoulders and clinging to me while I felt him.

I traced his back, feeling his lithe form through his clothes while he shook, then pressed my arm between us, forcing enough space to touch him properly, like I'd been aching to do since the brief feel of him against the back of my hand.

He gasped, his fingers digging into my back as though to steady himself.

"I need this off," I whispered roughly, tugging Latif's robe. A shiver ran through his body, but he pulled back.

In the glow from the pool, I watched appreciatively as he pulled the tie open. The fabric fell loose around him. Head still bowed, he pushed it off his shoulders, allowing it to fall around his ankles.

My mouth dried at the sight of him. What I could see in the soft glow was a perfect man, with a lean build, pale skin glowing, and iridescent scales that caught the light, all over, including around his long, smooth cock.

And he looked so nervous that I was surprised he was still standing here, facing me and what we were planning to do.

I stepped up to him, taking his trembling hands in mine.

"It's okay," I whispered. "We can stop if you want to."

He gripped mine tightly and shook his head, finally chancing a glance up to meet my eyes. His scared gaze went straight through me, and at that moment, I knew I would do anything he asked of me.

"Please don't stop."

I shut my eyes.

"Okay," I breathed, pulling him closer again. Our foreheads met and our gazes did next.

I tilted my chin up, but Latif shied away, so I didn't push it.

Instead, I gripped the waistband of my shorts and shoved them down.

Latif gasped.

"Can I touch it?" he whispered.

I chuckled breathlessly.

"You don't have to ask."

Swallowing, he reached out, gripping me eagerly, even though he was still trembling.

I shut my eyes, letting him explore my cock with slow, measured strokes.

Unable to stay still any longer, I reached for his cock in return.

He was big, but for his height, not intimidatingly so. Not that that mattered. I wouldn't say no to sucking dick, but I liked to top in general and Latif's ass...

I slid my hand down, eager to feel it, and was met with… a tail.

Before I knew what to think of that fact, it swung around, loosely hugging the backs of my ankles.

The small, affectionate gesture made me smile, even as my breath hitched under his touch.

Still on a mission, I slid my hand lower still, reaching beneath the base of his tail until I could finally feel his firm ass cheeks. I squeezed, and Latif groaned, promptly releasing me when his entire body twitched.

"Let me get you off," I whispered.

He nodded profusely.

"Yes," he gasped. "Please."

I tugged him closer and thrust my abandoned cock to his skin, need and desire flowing through me like fire.

"You smell so good," I moaned.

I wanted to make it good, to suck him off or fuck

him, but he was clinging to me like a life preserver and all I could do was continue to feel the silky-smooth skin of his cock against my palm.

I wrapped my hand around it and began to stroke the length.

"Oh. Oh Goddess," Latif gasped.

His legs were already shaking, and I easily supported his weight, holding him steady.

"Does it feel good?" I asked, and he moaned in response. "Yeah? Like this?"

It occurred to me that he probably didn't know *how* he liked it. After all, he said he normally meditated when he got turned on. So instead, I went by the noises he made, the way he gasped and cried out softly when I twisted my wrist as his tip.

With my other hand, I held his ass, squeezing a cheek while my finger delved further down and... he was *wet*.

It was unexpected but sexy as hell to feel the slippery liquid against my fingertip.

I ran my finger over his tight hole, feeling the muscles flex and just as I pressed it inside, Latif bucked in my arms. He pressed back, taking deeper, his muscles clenching my digit tightly. A wrecked moan tore from his lips and he suddenly pressed his face into my neck, inhaling sharply as he cried out again.

Come splattered against me, soaking my hand where I continued to pull his cock.

It throbbed against my palm and a sweet scent filled the air.

For a moment, I kept stroking him, my grip soft.

I hadn't pulled my other hand free either. I couldn't quite bring myself to withdraw from his hot heat.

I moaned softly, gently slipping in and out.

"I want to fuck you," I sighed.

Latif stilled, the post-orgasmic looseness of his body stiffening, giving me my answer. To be fair, I supposed, virgin to anal sex was a big leap.

"I won't," I said to reassure him, stroking his back soothingly. "I just *want* to."

Latif was still for a moment longer, only breathing against my neck.

"Can I do something else for you?" he asked and there was so much hesitance and worry in his voice that I finally released him properly and put my arms around his waist, just holding him.

"You can kiss me while I take care of *this*." I gently thrust forward so that he could feel what exactly I meant, but he stiffened even more.

"Or not. That's fine too."

"You said you don't like our bonding culture," Latif said, his voice full of accusation.

"Ah... I forgot about the kissing."

I chuckled. How could I forget *that* little detail? Explaining how humans frequently kissed each other to the alpha council months ago had been one of the most awkward conversations I'd ever had.

"Our human kisses don't make bonds," I explained.

"But they did with Alex and Saar and with Devin and Eisa too."

"I know," I reassured. "Just not amongst us humans, so I forgot for a moment. I happen to have a very distracting omega in my arms if you hadn't noticed. I'm not thinking clearly."

"Nor am I," Latif whispered. "Because I still want to touch you."

I shivered.

"You don't have to."

"I know. I just... I want to do it."

After a moment, his tentative fingers brushed my tip.

"It's wet," he whispered, gently rubbing the fluid around.

I shut my eyes, letting my head rest against his.

"Yeah, because you turned me on so much..."

That seemed to give him some confidence and he wrapped his hand around my cock, his grip surer this time.

"Like this?" he asked, already learning from me.

I reached down, letting my hand fall over his fist and showing him how I wanted it. Tight and slow.

My eyes nearly rolled at the sensation.

It had been way too long.

"That's it," I whispered.

I was already so on edge, so close that it only took a minute before I was coming with a groan, hips pumping into Latif's hand.

He gasped with me, lips parted as he watched my face hungrily.

Then he released me but stayed where he was while I caught my breath, still inhaling my scent softly.

"Is it my pheromones?" I asked.

"I want to bathe in them," Latif confirmed.

Despite having just finished, I reached down.

Sure enough, he was hard again.

"Want more?" I asked, but he shook his head.

"No. I can't even believe that I did that much."

Finally, he pulled back, avoiding my gaze as he reached for his discarded clothing.

"Can we go back now?" he asked, pulling them hastily back on.

Despite myself, I was a little disappointed. I couldn't help but want to hold him for a little bit longer.

It took a while to get presentable and then back track all the way to the entrance. Passing beneath all the watching faces this time, it felt like they were giving me judgmental looks.

"Hey, can you blame me?" I muttered.

"Hm?" Latif asked, glancing back at me.

I shook my head.

"Nothing."

It was with great relief that I finally saw the small tunnel we had entered through, if only because I could see the bright light from outside. I couldn't wait to get into it, lowering onto my belly without hesitation to crawl this time.

I had to squeeze my eyes shut as I reached the exit though, because the daylight was blinding after however long spent in the dark.

Once I was outside and standing upright, Latif emerged, immediately bumping into my back.

"Oops, sorry," he said, shielding his eyes.

To be safe on the rocky terrain, we sat down to wait for our eyes to adjust.

"You won't tell anyone, right?" Latif asked.

I reached out, taking his hand and squeezing it. To my pleasure, he didn't pull his away.

"I wouldn't kiss and tell—so to speak."

He smiled softly, giving me a look.

"You are obsessed with kissing," he informed me. "Your poison's effect must be all-encompassing."

"Poison?" I asked, confused.

"The aphrodisiac in your kiss," he said lightly.

He kicked a stone with his handle, humming thoughtfully.

"I can only imagine," he mused thoughtfully. "That was already quite a lot for me."

I sat still for a long moment as something clicked into place.

"There's an aphrodisiac in your saliva?" I asked carefully.

"Only in alphas, as far as I know," Latif said curiously. "Why? Don't humans have it too?"

I shook my head, thoughts racing.

For the first time, I felt like I finally understood why Alex had suddenly wanted his alien mate above all else.

He had been drugged.

ten

. . .

LATIF

Just before we went our separate ways on the path, Blaine's hand snagged mine again, stopping me.

I met his sharp eyes, marveling at the way one look from him alone made my blood rush.

"What is it?" I asked.

"Tomorrow," he said. And the word sounded just like a promise. "Is there anywhere else we can meet? I want to see more before we run out of time."

Disappointment filled me.

"Somewhere more comfortable hopefully..."

The suggestion in his voice made me bite my lip

as the disappointment was pushed out by pleased anticipation.

"The library," I found myself saying. "Meet me there at noon. I will try to take the room in the back left corner. If that one has been taken, I will take the one next to it."

"But can't anyone walk in?" he asked.

I shook my head, amazed that we were talking about this so openly. Like it really was okay for us to do.

"There are wooden doors so that the omegas can lock them."

He lifted his brows.

"I didn't know that those existed on Mukhana."

"For privacy in public places, yes."

He smiled softly and then reached out, gently brushing a strand of hair back from my face.

"See you at the library, then," he said.

I stood there, watching him walk away for far too long.

It was probably for the best that we moved somewhere cleaner. Blaine was covered in dirt from crawling through the cave. And his clothes were filthy from being discarded while we had...

I swallowed the thought away. I couldn't think about this now! Addy would be arriving to pick me up from the temple soon.

I hurried back, looking down at my own clothes as I went. They weren't too bad. The color hid some of the dirt. If anyone asked, I would say I had been cleaning the grounds.

I entered the path, rushing even more when I glanced up and saw how much time had really passed.

"Latif?"

The sound of Addy's voice stopped me in my tracks. I faltered, then spun around to see him, hurrying to reach me, his thick brows drawn into an angry frown.

"What are you doing out here?" he demanded.

"I—I didn't want to wait for you any longer, so I started down the path."

"The priest allowed that?" he demanded.

"No—I was just heading back because I forgot to say goodbye."

"Latif, you have to stop this," he chastised, grabbing me by the arm to lead me away. "You are *not* an alpha. You can't just walk around on your own."

I snatched my arm away.

"This is an omega area," I spat. "Very few unmated alphas even come here."

"*I'm* here, aren't I?"

"Yes, but you're my brother."

He groaned.

"That's not—" He sighed heavily. "Just be quiet and come home."

"Fine," I muttered and used my anger with him as an excuse to bypass both of my parents, who were sitting in the kitchen talking, Al-mother's ankle resting on a chair.

"How was the temple?" Om-father asked.

"Fine!" I shouted on the way to my room.

"What did you say?" Al-mother demanded.

Addy began to argue at once, but I pulled my thick curtains closed and tuned out the sound of their discussion.

I was used to them talking about me as though I wasn't there, anyway. Not like Blaine. He seemed to hang on my every word, just as I did his.

Swallowing, I went to the window and leaned on it to look outside. I didn't see a thing, just his gorgeous eyes, watching me while pleasure coursed through his body, his member in my hand.

He had made me see stars, and I had given him an orgasm too.

Despite my nerves, he had been so kind about it. So passionate. He'd wanted more... I'd intended to do everything, but at the last moment fear had seized me.

There's still tomorrow, I thought, and a shiver ran through me.

His body was so enticing. Surprisingly, he had light hair where I hadn't expected it. For some reason, I'd wanted to press my face into it... probably for the same reason I'd pressed my nose into his neck. He smelled so good, and it aroused me more than anything I'd ever experienced.

"Latif? I brought you some food."

Drawn from my thoughts, I looked over my shoulder to find Om-father carrying in a platter of fresh fruit.

Swallowing, I went and took it from him, taking it to the table to eat.

"Are you okay?" he asked quietly. "Did something happen?"

I paused, then lowered myself purposely into the chair. For a moment, I'd thought he knew, but how could he?

"Nothing happened other than Addy being rude, as usual. He grabbed my arm too hard."

Om-father tutted and examined where I gestured.

"It's fine," I insisted. "He just annoyed me."

Om-father nodded but he still looked worried.

"And Blaine?" he asked, his voice even lower.

"He's okay," I said. "A bit boring."

Relief passed over Om-father's face.

"He really has not touched you?" he asked. "Because I feel terrible for putting you in this position. I don't know what I was thinking. Having you bound is not worth your safety. I don't want you to go tomorrow."

Stunned, I looked up at Om-father.

"I thought the auction was the most important thing in the world for you," I said slowly, and he seemed to deflate.

"Latif, the only thing I really care about is your happiness," he said, frowning. "I thought the auctions would give you something that you are seeking but I seemed to have lost my mind sending you around with that human."

I did not know what to say. If he only knew what I had been doing this afternoon.

"You didn't send me out there with just any alpha," I reminded him. "Blaine is human. He does not have to act on his pheromones. And don't worry, he canceled the rest of the meetings," I added. "He said he saw enough of the caves."

It was the truth and it seemed to comfort him, but it only filled me with guilt.

"I'm glad," he said firmly. "Please forgive me, Latif."

I chuckled but there was an edge to it that I hoped my om-father didn't notice.

"There's nothing to be sorry for," I insisted. "I

went around the caves for a couple of hours. Told him about the creation story, and then came home."

Om-father let out a small sigh and reached out, patting my hand.

"I shall talk to your mother about the classes," he said, smiling.

"Really?" I asked.

"Yes, love."

He pressed a kiss to the top of my head and then paused.

"You smell like him," he informed me.

I froze.

"Hm. Maybe that's why Addy was so overprotective of you today."

"Maybe," I managed.

I waited with bated breath for Om-father to leave my room before collapsing in relief.

My heart was pounding so hard.

If I met with Blaine tomorrow, I would have to bring something to mask his scent afterward. Today I had been lucky.

For the rest of the day, I fluctuated between shock over what I had done and fear of ever trying it again. I half thought of not turning up to our meeting tomorrow, but I did not know who I was trying to fool.

We hadn't done what I wanted today.

I wanted Blaine inside me so badly that it almost hurt. I wanted to squeeze his alpha length deep inside me instead of his fingers. Goddess help me, I wanted to sit on his lap and feel how far inside he would go.

It was like some sort of hypnosis had occurred. With each touch, I wanted more. I had felt Blaine's hand against my erection and had wanted us naked. Then, I had felt his fingertip inside me and now I craved his whole erection.

When would it stop?

As morning came and I woke from fitful dreams, I wasn't sure I had the strength to do anything but beg for what I wanted.

It took everything in me to wait until almost noon before asking and, to my chagrin, Om-father and Al-mother were gone when I emerged to do so.

"Where are our parents?" I asked.

"Out for a walk," Addy informed me.

He was sitting in the living room, sharpening his longsword.

From what I'd heard whispered, only cowards and bad fighters used weapons, but Addy seemed to care more about winning than being honorable.

"Does that mean Al-mother's foot has healed?" I asked.

He shrugged.

"I suppose so."

I watched him for a moment before looking out the smoke escape. The sun was almost directly above it.

"Can you take me to the library?" I asked.

Addy finally stopped what he was doing and looked at me. I didn't blame him; I never asked him for favors.

"Why? You have plenty of books."

"I've read them all too many times."

He continued to stare at me.

"Trust me, I would go on my own if I could."

To my surprise, he pursed his lips and stood.

"Come on."

I tried not to let my relief show.

Not wanting to start another bickering match, I followed him quietly through the streets.

The library was a bit of a sanctuary. It was huge and filled with books and old scrolls. I loved the atmosphere as we entered the large stone building, but as usual, I wished that I could simply walk the stacks myself. Instead, as an unmated omega, I was required to pick from the catalog from the safety of the back rooms.

Addy led me straight to the corner room. It was my usual one.

We knocked on the door, but no one answered.

After a moment, I tried the handle, finding it unlocked and unoccupied.

Within, there was a large table for studying on, a bench to sit on, and of course, the catalog system.

There was a window too, but it was high enough that no one could look in.

Excitement bubbled within me.

"Okay, I'm good now, thank you," I said, nearly closing the door in Addy's face.

"Wait, how much time do you need?"

"Oh, a few hours at least," I said quickly. "Give me three."

"Three hours?" he demanded. "To pick a book?"

"I'll read while I'm here," I argued. "I've been stuck in the house for too long."

He sighed heavily.

"Fine, I'll be back then."

I slammed the door shut.

Normally, I locked it immediately, but this time, I left it unlocked and backed up to the table, leaning back against it, tail swishing anxiously.

I couldn't even bring myself to look at the catalog. The thick book with all the titles was sitting open next to the book chute. All I had to do was ring the right number through the system of strings and a few minutes later, my book would be delivered directly to the room. Wrapped up and safe and ready to be read.

Instead of browsing though, I stood where I was, unable to tear my gaze from the door.

It felt like an eternity before the handle finally began to turn and when the door pushed open. When Blaine snuck through the narrow opening, I couldn't stop myself from moving to him.

I didn't know what came over me, but I didn't say a word, just forced my way into his arms, pressing my face to his neck again and practically *melting*.

"Did you miss me?" Blaine chuckled and oh, that breathless laugh of his did something to me.

"Lock the door," I whispered.

Blaine swallowed and turned, clicking the lock into place before turning back around, heat in his gaze so intense that I could barely face it.

We didn't need to say anything. He stepped up to me, bending and lifting me by the thighs. Without thinking, I moved my tail aside and spread my legs around his waist as he lowered me onto the table.

He was already hard, his erection digging into my own and his hands frantically pulling my robe up to my waist then kicking his clothes off.

I was still nervous. My heart was racing but it was more with arousal than fear this time.

He stepped up against me, overwhelming me

with the sinfully delicious feeling of our lengths rubbing together.

His lips suddenly landed on my neck, kissing me there and my jaw and all over and I hadn't expected someone's lips to feel so soft and sensual, especially with the slightly rough slide of stubble accompanying them.

"I need you," I gasped.

"You've got me," he answered.

"Not like yesterday," I found myself whispering. "Inside me."

He paused and drew back to look at me, but I was already dripping wet and clenching on nothing.

I needed this more than air and he must have seen that on my face, because suddenly, he pushed my knees up so that I had to lean back on my hands.

Gasping, I caught myself and stared in shock at Blaine while he looked at me. I had never been so exposed to anyone before, not even yesterday in the cave. Now, perched on top of a table with my legs spread, knees practically to my chest while he watched me, I found it exhilarating. He groaned at the sight of me, desire obvious in his expression.

"Oh, God, Latif," he breathed, and then, without any other warning, he bent down, pressing his lips to the ring of muscles there.

I gasped, squirming for a moment, but he held

my legs up firmly. When his tongue delved inside, I cried out. Then, to stop myself from making too much noise, I clamped a hand over my mouth, falling back flat on the table.

My head was only half on the surface, but I didn't care about anything other than the tongue inside me. It felt *good*. Better than fingers.

I gasped, arching down for more, my whole body moving as though possessed, hips chasing the feeling.

Blaine was moaning, nearly as loud as I was, and suddenly fingers joined, pressing inside me while his tongue stroked the outside.

I was shaking and on the edge of this ending far too soon, but I couldn't find any words to tell him that. Nothing but gasps and soft cries left my lips.

His tongue paused then, but the fingers kept going, bringing me even closer before suddenly, they were removed, replaced by something else.

I hadn't noticed him repositioning over me, so the feeling of his large, hard length penetrating my hole tore a gasp from my throat.

I lifted my head, watching in shock as he pressed slowly but surely into me.

He moaned as he filled me, his gaze darkened by desire and he reached for me, pressing a wet finger into my mouth, spreading the taste of my own slick across my tongue.

Pleasure burst through me. My hole clenched around him. I barely had time to reach down and grasp my length before stars exploded before my eyes and I came, writhing on his hard length.

"No," I gasped. "No. No. *No.*"

I squeezed my eyes shut against the onslaught of emotions that accosted me, but suddenly, there were gentle hands on my cheeks.

"Latif," Blaine whispered. "What is it? What's wrong, baby?"

Being treated as an omega my whole life was bad enough. Being called a baby while I had an alpha buried within me was even worse. But that was something I would address later. For now, I was too upset to think of anything but the travesty that had happened.

"I wanted to do this so badly." My voice broke, but I forced it out. "I couldn't stop myself from ending it too soon."

Blaine tilted my chin up, forcing me to meet his serious gaze.

"Latif, we are far from done here."

A chill of anticipation traveled over my skin.

Without breaking eye contact, he slowly pulled out and then took his time sliding back in.

"Feel that?" he asked. "It's not going anywhere yet."

I took a ragged breath, nodding.

"Okay," I whispered.

eleven

. . .

I kept my movements slow and steady, pressing in deep and pulling out slowly until his cock was getting hard again.

He was hugging his knees, his eyes squeezed shut, lips parted. We'd been in such a rush we hadn't even undressed. I'd only kicked my pants down and hoisted up his robes. Even his feet were still in sandals, the fabric wrinkling under him, the edges wet from where his come has splashed.

I had never in my life seen anything so beautiful. Possessiveness surged unexpectedly through me, and I shuddered, my cock flexing inside him.

Latif gasped and reached for his cock, gripping the wet length in his elegant hand.

I stilled, taking a moment to breathe through the overwhelming pleasure of having him under me, his hole sopping wet and tighter than a fist.

Only when I took one of his ankles in my hand did Latif's eyes flutter open. He looked at me through a haze of desire, his blue eyes nearly black.

Without speaking, I pulled the sandal gently off his foot. I didn't know what I had been planning, other than to undress him further, but instead, I pressed the arch of his foot to my lips.

He stilled, watching me as I kissed the smooth skin, dragging my lips to the toes.

Suddenly, he began to pump his fist over his cock faster, watching me raptly. His entire body shuddered when he came, and I rode him through the wave, groaning at the feeling, his ankle still clasped in my hand.

This time, when he was finished, I didn't give him recovery time.

I pulled out quickly, but I was too wound up.

"Get up," I said gruffly.

Shaking like a baby lamb, Latif pushed up on his hands.

I helped him out of his robe and got him on his feet, holding him steady by the hips.

"Turn around," I instructed, finally pulling my shirt off.

It was hot in here. Who was I kidding, the planet was always hot everywhere. It felt good to have the fresh air on my bare skin because just underneath felt like fire. Sweat clung to my skin and hair, and my cock was so hard that it ached.

"I need to get back inside you," I whispered.

He nodded shakily and turned around, like I'd told him.

I gently pushed his back down, and he got the idea at once and gripped onto the edge of the table for support while I took his hips in my hands.

I pushed into him, perhaps too hard, because he cried out, bucking against me.

Holding his hips in place, I couldn't stop myself this time. I pounded into his wet ass, groaning gutturally as he took me in, pushing back to meet each thrust.

"Yes," he hissed and that was all it took for me to finally lose the control I had. I fucked him hard, skin slapping, fingers digging into his skin until I was losing all sense of rhythm.

I shoved in deep, one last time, emptying within him.

He gasped, pressing back as hard as he could, writhing against my cock.

"Oh," he moaned, "oh Goddess. That feels so good."

He pumped back against me while my cock flexed inside him, and we both groaned this time.

"Just don't knot me," he whispered.

Fuck. I'd forgotten about that minuscule detail. Latif could get pregnant...

"I don't have a knot," I said, waiting for the news to sink in while I stroked his smooth back, lingering on the sleek scales. They were almost slippery to the touch and so beautiful the way they shimmered like water.

"What does that mean?" Latif finally asked.

"It means you have to push it out," I said gently.

Carefully, I pulled out. We both shuddered, but I pressed a hand to Latif's lower back, keeping him down.

"Push," I whispered.

I felt hesitation in the line of his back, but after a moment, his wet hole flexed and then a gush of thick cream spilled free.

The sight made me moan, something primal and hungry pulsing through me.

"Yeah," I groaned. "Like that. Keep pushing."

More spurted free, dripping over his already wet cheeks and I couldn't deny myself any longer. I pressed my lips to his wetness, lapping him clean with my tongue, my masculine taste mingling with his sweet omega honey.

When I finally lifted, it felt like I was high. I was dazed.

Latif was bent in half, completely flat on the table, clutching the edges with white knuckles, his chest heaving.

For a moment, I almost felt bad, but he had wanted this. He had started it. And he had liked every moment of it.

"Come here," I said and helped to lift him, gently maneuvering him to the bench that we hadn't touched.

I tucked him against my side, pressing kisses to his temple and hair while he nuzzled my neck again.

He was shivering from what we had done and from my fingers rubbing the back of his neck.

I pressed them into his hair, massaging the back of his skull until he sagged fully against me.

Now in the afterglow, a smile pulled my lips.

I was pretty sure I was supposed to be on a mission. Saving the omegas or something. God, it was a pressing issue and all, but I couldn't imagine anything being more important than this sweet alien man in my arms right now.

I squeezed him in closer.

"I can't believe we did that," he said, voice low

and reverent.

I hummed thoughtfully, still playing with his hair.

"How do you feel?"

"Sleepy," he decided.

I smiled.

"When are you going to be picked up? Do you have time for a nap?"

Latif stilled and lifted his head to search my face.

"Do you wish to rest now?" he asked. "Because I told my brother to leave me for three hours."

My mouth went dry.

"Do you mean you want more?"

I glanced down, seeing his soft cock.

"This is the last time we can do this," he said quietly. "I want to use every moment of our time."

He bit his lip, gazing at me through those thick lashes, and my cock twitched with renewed interest.

"You're going to have to stop doing that if you don't want me to kiss you," I warned, cupping his cheek and pulling his lip gently from his teeth with my thumb.

I rubbed the soft fullness, enthralled, before his lips parted gently.

"Can I taste it again?" he asked against my finger, lids heavy as he watched me.

I nodded, pressing my thumb between his lips.

"Suck," I whispered.

His eyes widened in surprise, but he did it, and a moment later, they fluttered shut in pleasure.

"You can suck me here, too," I informed him, and his eyes flew open to see me holding my cock for him.

His lips parted in a silent "O," but he simply pulled my finger out and bent his head down.

The first touch of his mouth was almost too sensitive, but quickly turned to pleasure as his soft mouth wrapped around the head.

Without instruction, he started to suck. I shut my eyes, head falling back while he explored me with his mouth.

It didn't take long to get hard again, and as I did, he began to moan, sucking me sloppier as it got bigger, filling him in a new way.

"Mm," I moaned, resting my hand on the back of his head, accidentally putting too much pressure there. He coughed and pulled back up.

He met my gaze and his was so hazy that I winced with sympathy. His eyes were empty of everything but overwhelming desire, and he fell back down against my cock like it was magnetic, licking the length hungrily and moaning before pressing his face to my base, inhaling like my scent was oxygen.

I was breathing hard, trying to let him have his fun this time. It took clenching the edges of the bench to stay still. I wanted to flip him and fuck him again, but he scrambled clumsily to his knees, straddling me.

I thought he was going to just go for it, using my cock in every way he needed it, but he paused, hesitance flying into his eyes.

"Can I sit on it?" he asked in a small voice.

I groaned, eyes rolling shut as I took a breath and precome shot from the tip.

"Fuck," I breathed. "Do it. Take what you want, Latif. I'm yours."

Something vibrant flew into his eyes and he sat back, taking my cock all the way down, crying out as he did, but not stopping.

He started to ride me without pause, rocking back and forth so hard that the bench was smacking the wall and I had to grab onto him to hold on.

He was mewling now, his face crunched with pleasure as he got close.

I looked down, just in time to see his cock spit come onto my stomach while he shuddered, and his thighs shook.

I held him tightly through it, moaning encouragement as he clenched and spasmed around me. Then, to my amazement, he took a trembling breath and gripped my shoulders for leverage as he started to ride me again.

"More," he whispered, his voice guttural from the shouting. "I don't want to stop."

I grunted, holding on for dear life until I was coming again, my cock soaking wet in our combined fluids.

He gasped, using his muscles to clench around me as he moved, milking out every last drop until he whimpered weakly, shaking as he came, and finally collapsed against me.

Gasps and soft cries left his lips until our bodies finally started to calm.

When I came back to reality, he was still sitting with me buried inside, curled up in a ball in my arms.

Aside from those long legs of his, he fit in my embrace so perfectly. Just the right fit for me to hold.

"What have I done," he whispered quietly into my neck.

I tilted his face toward mine, surprised by his anguished expression.

"What's wrong?" I asked.

He squeezed his eyes tightly shut.

"Blaine," he mumbled. "How am I to go back to living without this?"

I tried not to laugh but my chest rumbled with it, and I threw my head back, chuckling.

Latif slapped my chest lightly, his face pinched in an adorable pout.

"It's not funny," he snapped. "You can just have sex whenever you want but I never can again."

I swallowed as the reality of his words struck me.

"Latif, I'm sorry. You're so right. It's not fair."

"Yes," he agreed, crossing his arms. "It isn't fair. Nothing in my life is."

He seemed suddenly so perturbed by it all that I pulled him against my chest again, squeezing him tightly.

"I'm sorry," I said.

He shook his head.

"Why? You did nothing."

"I'm still sorry. It's not fair for you or any other omega."

"Is that really how you feel?" he asked.

At my nod, he took a deep breath, releasing it slowly. All the tension seeped out of him again.

"Oh Blaine," he sighed. "Maybe this doesn't have to be the only time. We can meet here again."

"Just tell me when and I'll be here."

"Tomorrow?" he asked tentatively. "At the same time?"

At my nod, he snuggled in closer. I could feel the smile on his lips, pressed to my shoulder.

And then there was a loud, jarring knock at the

door.

Latif gasped, bolting straight up.

We stared at each other in shock while someone began to rattle the door. Then Addy's voice carried to us.

"Latif? Are you in there? Open up."

Latif practically jumped off my lap.

Immediately, we both paused to wince at the feeling of him jumping off my cock so carelessly.

"Sorry," he hissed.

"Latif?" Addy said from the other side. "Open the door!"

"C-coming!"

To my chagrin, he almost *did* run to the door to open it, clearly not thinking, because he was buck naked, soaked in come and slick, and I was in here in a similar state. I grabbed him by the arm, swinging him away from the door and silently shoving his clothing into his arms.

Eyes wide, he took the robes, fighting into the fabric.

I would have helped normally, but I was struggling into my shirt and pants.

"Out the window!" Latif whispered frantically, shoving me toward it.

Without hesitating I jumped onto the bench to reach it, gripped the edge, and hoisted myself over.

The window was smaller than I expected, but Addy's knocks had turned frantic.

"What are you doing in there?!" he demanded. "Open the damn door, Latif! This isn't funny!"

"One second!"

Just as I fell through the opening, I heard the lock open.

I hit the ground in a not very graceful way, landing pretty much on my shoulder and then rolling to fall flat on the ground.

Instead of moving, I lay there, listening to the sounds from inside, heart pounding and body aching from the fall.

"Was someone in here?" Addy was demanding loudly. Shit... the sound really carried. Had we even *tried* to be quiet?"

"Are you alright?" someone asked.

I lifted my head, finding another pretty omega watching me with wide yellow eyes.

"I'm fine," I insisted and forced myself up, walking hastily away.

Only when I reached the corner did I look back, and my heart clenched at the sight of nassa eyes watching me from across the street.

Countless people had seen me...

But Addy hadn't. That was all that mattered, I told myself.

twelve

. . .

LATIF

The moment the lock was opened, Addy marched through, practically bowling me out of the way.

I stood back against the wall, trembling as Addy circled the room like an animal on the hunt.

Finally, he stopped in the middle and turned to face me head-on.

I was shaking and he saw it at once. He knew that I was never scared of him. We bickered, but he would never hurt me. I knew that, and he knew that. Perhaps that was why such a fire burned in his eyes.

"Was someone in here with you?" he asked slowly.

I shook my head frantically.

I knew I must look like a mess because my hair flew free of the ties all around my face.

"I heard you talking to someone."

It took me a moment to find my voice.

"I wasn't talking to anyone."

Addy's fists clenched.

"Latif. The room reeks of *alpha*."

I swallowed, unable to meet his suspicious eyes.

"Does it?"

I had brought incense and perfume to mask the scent this time, but I had forgotten all about it in the mad rush to get the door open before too much time had passed.

"I did notice that when I first entered," I lied. "There must have been an alpha using this room before me."

Addy was silent for a long time.

When I chanced a look up, his gaze was fixed on my bag that had been discarded in the middle of the floor.

I had forgotten to pick it up. And next to it, a splash of liquid, either from me or Blaine, I couldn't be sure. The sight of it nearly made my heart stop. There was a chance that the strap of my bag was covering it from Addy's angle, but I shook like a leaf in the wind waiting for him to say something.

"So you were just reading in here, like normal. With no one visiting you when they shouldn't?" he asked.

It felt like a trap, but I could not think of a thing to do other than nod.

"That's right."

"Latif," Addy growled. "Then where are your books?"

I blinked.

My lips parted in shock, mostly because, until now, I often thought of my brother as dim-witted. Yet here he was outsmarting me.

Only because I was in such a panic, I told myself. I just had to remain calm. Addy had no proof of anything. All he had was a hunch, really.

"To be honest, I fell asleep," I found myself saying. "I didn't read a thing."

His gaze narrowed.

"You fell asleep?" he repeated incredulously. "You really expect me to believe that?"

"What else do you think happened?" I demanded. "You think that an alpha was in here? Doing what exactly?"

He blinked at me.

"I'm not bonded. You would know that straight away."

What he didn't know was that I could be intimate

with others the way that he could not. I was counting on that little bit of power to win me this argument. After a moment spent waiting with bated breath, I watched as he pursed his lips and shrugged.

"I guess that's true," he said, but he still watched me with narrow eyes. Then, to my chagrin, he turned and went to the bench, climbing onto it to look outside.

I took the opportunity to whip up my bag, wiping the come off the floor with the bottom of my sandal.

"I don't think anyone can climb in through there," I said lightly.

Addy huffed in response.

"Whatever," he muttered. "Let's go."

It should have felt like a win, but it didn't.

It felt like everyone could tell.

Before even leaving the library, I caught several curious eyes on me.

I was being paranoid. How could they know?

"Can you take me to the bathhouse instead of home?" I asked.

Addy glared at me. "No," he snapped. "I have to meet my friends soon."

"Please, Addy, you said that room stank of alpha. I probably reek of whoever it was."

He groaned and turned at the next street.

"I won't be long," I said, hurrying to the omega

entrance as we reached it and nearly stumbling into Alil and his om-mother.

"Oh, Latif."

"Hi," I mumbled and, even though it wasn't like me, I rushed past them to the door. They both exchanged a look with Addy, who shrugged sullenly.

"Meet you inside!" I said, trying for a friendly smile, but once I *was* inside, I lost all sense of decorum. I hurried to the nearest showering point, paying no attention to anyone around me as I frantically undressed and began to scrub myself clean.

It wasn't until I had scrubbed every inch of my body that I felt like I could breathe again. I stood under the spray, eyes closed, just trying to calm down.

Everything about that had been far too close.

Addy had known. If he was any bit smarter than he was, he would have figured it out. But his experience with the world was limited in its own way. Like the omegas, there were things he didn't understand. Like an unmated omega and an unmated alpha riding each other for hours in a library.

I swallowed as goosebumps traveled over my skin.

Every stolen moment had been amazing. But it had been just as dangerous. I did not know what would be done to us if anyone found out, but we had nearly let that happen.

If I had gone straight home the way I had planned, I was sure that Om-father would have figured it out at once. After all, I was not supposed to have seen Blaine today, yet his scent had been all over me, in every intimate crevice and curve of my body.

"What is that?"

Startled, I glanced over, finding Alil next to me, water cascading over him.

"Hm?"

He gestured to my hips, and I glanced down, dumbfounded for a moment at the sight of clear handprints bruised into my skin.

"It's from training," I found myself saying, but Alil frowned.

"But you keep missing practice," he said slowly. "We all thought you were in trouble."

I forced a laugh.

"Yes. I am. I'm not allowed back for now, so I was trying to show Addy the moves. He's so clumsy."

Alil smiled softly.

"He's not much of a fighter, is he?" he asked. "Far too gentle, you can tell from a mile away."

I gave Alil an incredulous look.

"More like he has no coordination," I argued.

He chuckled lightly but dropped it, turning back to cleaning himself.

I stepped from the water, drying myself quickly, wishing that I had brought a change of clothes. If this had been planned, I would have.

"Would you like to come sit in the pool and chat?" Alil asked.

I glanced over. It was busy there today. The hot pools were filled with omegas. With our population shrinking, I knew that they were mostly mated ones, and I had a suspicion that any of them would know what these bruises were *really* from.

I shook my head regretfully.

"Sorry, I'm still in trouble. I am supposed to go straight home."

Alil hummed thoughtfully.

"I understand. My family would have been furious if I got so close to an unmated alpha like that."

I winced. I could only imagine what they would do if they found out the truth.

"Exactly," I muttered and then bid him farewell, moving back to the benches by the entrance to wait.

It didn't take long for Om-father to open it and find me there.

"Done already?" he asked. "I thought I would join you for a dip."

"You can go if you want," I said, "but I will wait here."

Om-father shook his head.

"I just thought it would be nice for us to talk," he said. "Oh well, another time."

He held the door open for me and we began to walk.

It wasn't until we were nearly home that I realized the walk had been silent. I looked at Om-father and found him watching me closely.

"Addy said some things when he came home," he said gently.

"Did he?" I asked, anxiety striking me again.

"Yes. That your room smelled like an alpha and that you were acting strange and wouldn't answer the door... Was it Blaine?" he asked when I did not speak.

I shook my head frantically.

"No, I just fell asleep."

"And the alpha scent?"

"Was just lingering, I suppose," I said weakly.

Om-father looked away.

"I thought maybe you were still helping him with his work but did not want me to worry."

"Oh."

If only I had thought of that.

"But then you rushed to the bathhouse so my

mind was going wild with worry until I remembered that Blaine is unmated and can't... you know, take advantage. At least, not with more than a kiss."

"Yes," I agreed. "And I am still not bound, so you have nothing to worry about."

The lies were coming far too easily now.

I didn't like it and I didn't want to keep saying them.

All of this was too close.

I couldn't meet Blaine tomorrow the way I wanted to.

Accepting that thought resolutely, I went through the rest of the day feeling numb and distant. I was living a huge, life-changing experience, and no one knew. At least with Devin's classes, I could discuss it with friends. Keeping this to myself was making me antsy. Especially because I was sure that someone would suddenly come out and say it. Maybe one of those in the library had heard our passionate cries and knew what we had been doing.

When Addy returned home in the evening, his eyes seemed to hold secrets in them. All night, he rarely looked at me, but when he did, it was with confusion and suspicion in his fiery gaze.

Unable to take it any longer, I excused myself to my room.

It had been amazing but, like all good things, it had to come to an end.

"Never again," I whispered aloud.

I fell asleep with that repeating in my head.

And I woke in the morning with my hard member in my hand and Blaine's name on my lips and I knew I would do whatever I had to, tell any lie I needed to, to get to him again today.

When I said I wanted to go to the library again, no one argued, but there was a strange air in the room.

Without a word, Al-mother stood to take me.

She did not speak until we were outside, putting an arm around my shoulders as we walked.

"You are a good omega," she said.

I glanced up at her.

"What does that mean?"

She smiled down at me kindly, gently rubbing my shoulder comfortingly, and foreboding filled me.

"Some people are saying things about you," she said, "but I do not believe them."

She glanced back over her shoulders, shooting a glare behind us.

My heart suddenly racing, I followed her look, just in time to see Addy duck around a corner. He had the stealth of a newborn Zalla.

"What is he doing?" I asked. "Why is he following us?"

"Because he's a fool who believes the rumors. But you wouldn't—"

"What rumors?" I choked.

"It doesn't matter," Al-mother said through gritted teeth. "I know you better. It's because of that fight you had. With the alpha. Now people are saying you've done even more inappropriate things with him."

I was shaking my head. I felt like I was about to be sick.

"But—"

I cut off the *how* on the tip of my tongue.

"It doesn't matter," Al-mother said fiercely. "I will protect you from anything. Even ugly words."

This was not good.

Blaine was going to come into the library to meet me. It was too in the open. We had been too loud. It would confirm everything.

Shame and humiliation filled me.

"Al-mother," I said, voice trembling. "I want to go home. I don't wish to face anyone today."

She shook her head.

"No, Latif. Go. Show them they are wrong."

Every eye in the library turned to me when we entered.

They pretended that they did not watch, but they all did. Everyone *always* watched. They always kept everyone in their place. Like the banks of a river, directing the flow of water. My life was like that. Flowing toward what was expected of me, without the ability to stop.

"Please, Al-mother," I whispered, but the desperation was too apparent in my voice and Al-mother's expression hardened, understanding filling her eyes.

"Get in that room, Latif," she said in a low voice. "Let me see if someone comes to visit you."

Shaking, I pushed the door open and slipped inside, slamming it shut behind me.

My heart felt like it was about to burst from the panic. I had to warn Blaine somehow. Perhaps I would see his approach from the window... Except it was far too late for that.

I gasped at the sight of him, already here waiting for me. The warm smile fell from his face, and he stood at once when I spun around to shove the lock into place.

"What's wrong?" he asked, coming to me.

I couldn't find words. I could barely breathe as he pulled me into a comforting embrace.

My stiff body couldn't relax but I couldn't push him off either, so I stood there, stricken with worry as he kissed my cheeks.

"We've been caught," I finally managed to choke.

Blaine stopped dead.

"What? What do you mean?"

"My al-mother is standing just outside the door waiting to see if anyone comes in."

Understanding crossed his expression. For a moment, he shut his eyes. Then, with those reassuring hands, he tugged my face down, pressing our foreheads together.

"What do you want to do?" he asked, searching my eyes.

"Oh, Goddess. Everyone already saw you enter. They all know we are here together now. It's only a matter of time before someone tells Al-mother."

Blaine nodded.

"Yeah," he whispered. "So, what do you want to do?"

I froze, finally seeing him. Even when my decision could lead to him being harmed, he let me choose and would follow me.

My hands lifted, fingers touching the smooth lines of his face. He'd shaved. How strange to be so close to someone, to feel their breath on your lips and see their heart in their actions, and to know that they were about to be torn away from you.

"We should face them," I whispered.

A soft smile touched his lips like he'd thought I should say that from the start.

"Now?" he asked gently.

At my nod, he took my hand, clasping it tightly before we unlocked the door.

thirteen

. . .

BLAINE

I wasn't about to leave Latif to face this alone. No way.

We had been naughty together, so we would face detention together too.

On the other hand, being slashed across the face by long, sharp claws had never been my punishment at school before.

I barely had time to register the people on the other side of the door before I was being attacked. The slash across the face came first, followed by a kick to the gut that sent me flying back.

I hit the ground, shock reverberating through me,

and for a moment saw stars. Then someone started to shout in pain.

"Latif!" someone growled. "Release him!"

I sat up at once and stared in astonishment at Latif kneeling on his brother's back, his arm twisted behind his back.

"If either of you touch Blaine again, I'll rip his arm out of its socket!"

I'd never heard that voice from him before, raw and filled with desperation and anger. He twisted a little bit in emphasis.

Addy cried out in pain, and Latif's al-mother immediately stepped forward.

"Release him!"

"Promise you won't touch Blaine!" Latif cried.

"Alright! Just let your brother go!"

He released him at once but did not wait to see if he was okay. Instead, he scrambled to my side, worried gaze on my cheek before he spun around to face the others.

I pushed to my feet behind him, seeing the way his al-mother turned disappointed eyes to us and his brother glared. There were others too. More nassa than I could count crowded the doorway, watching the scene. As nosy as ever, it seemed. But then I saw that one of them was Latif's om-father and my heart sank.

He stared at us with the most betrayed eyes I had ever had directed at me, and even though he was not *my* father, I still wanted to beg his forgiveness.

But Latif lifted his chin and remained silent until, finally, there was another commotion.

A moment later, Alya, from the alpha council, forced her way to the front of the crowd. Glancing around at all of us, she turned, tugged Latif's om-father into the room, and shut the door to block out the onlookers.

"What has happened here?" she asked, but her gaze lingered on me and Latif, so she could probably guess.

"That human has defiled my child," Latif's al-mother choked.

"It was my choice," Latif said. I could tell he wanted to sound strong and sure, but the effect was ruined by the tremble in his voice. I stepped out from behind him, putting my arm around his shoulders. *Fuck it.* They already knew. No point in pretending we hadn't done it now, not when Latif needed me. Sure enough, he leaned into my touch. I could feel his heart pounding against my arm.

"This is all my fault," his om-father whispered.

"What are you talking about?" his mate demanded.

"I-I allowed them to secretly work together. I

thought the humans were different. I didn't know their alphas could—"

"How could you do that?!" his al-mother demanded.

"Latif said that he would do the auctions if I allowed it!"

He turned, facing me, his expression twisted with betrayal.

"I trusted you!" he shouted.

That may as well have been a knife in the gut. The only weak argument that I had slipped from my lips.

"I didn't *bond* with him, though," I said. "That's got to count for something, right?"

The way they all stared at me said otherwise.

"Come," Alya finally said. "Let us continue this discussion in the council building, where it won't be overheard."

She paused, looking at Addy.

"Do you require medical attention?"

He was nursing his arm, which looked inflamed, even from the other side of the room. But he shook his head, jaw clenched.

If Alya had wanted privacy for us, I didn't see how our sorry parade through the streets could possibly be a good thing.

It felt like half the city got to see firsthand what it looked like when an omega was being disgraced.

I almost wanted to tell Latif to go and walk with his parents, to make it less apparent what was happening. But he was walking so close to my side that I couldn't do it. He wasn't looking at me, his face turned down, eyes on the path, but I could still tell he was taking comfort from me being next to him.

Meanwhile, I could feel the daggers being pointed at my back by his family who walked behind us.

Honestly, I understood.

To the nassa, I was the big bad wolf humans warned their children about. I'd lured him. Deflowered him... Don't get me started on societies that valued purity over freedom... Yes, Latif had wanted to do it. I hadn't forced him to sit on my cock and ride me like his life depended on it, but that was beside the point. The problem was that I hadn't stopped him. I probably should have, but I couldn't bring myself to regret it now.

As we entered the council building, I was flooded with unpleasant memories. That night, sitting with the alpha council, growing more and more uneasy because of Saar's behavior... Then watching him get stolen and carried out *that* very roof.

I looked up at the hole, amazed that Saar had cleared it *with* a whole person in his arms.

I had to swallow down the emotions that rushed through me at that. Coming here of all places to talk was a bad idea. Being in here to discuss another omega who didn't have a say in what happened to him was making my stomach hurt.

"Please, sit," Alya said. "It should not take long for the others to arrive."

We all did. Watching each other in silence around the large table.

Latif's om-father still looked crushed. I couldn't meet his eyes, and neither could Latif.

I reached under the table, taking his hand. He squeezed it at once, shooting me a grateful glance.

Alya was correct. I wasn't sure how they knew to come here, but it only took a minute for the members of the alpha council to begin to filter through the door.

"Will you go fetch the others?" Head Alpha Kion asked one of the alphas after entering. "They must not have heard."

He nodded and left while the rest came to take seats around us.

Kion took the head of the table.

"Now, who would like to tell me what happened?"

"Latif was acting like a brat," Addy said, jumping in at once. "He insisted that I take him to the library yesterday and didn't want to wait for anyone else to take him. He said he wanted three hours there, which is a long time, right?"

He looked around as though expecting everyone to nod. I could spend far more time in a library than three hours, so I kept my mouth shut.

"Go on," Alya instructed.

"When I got there to take him home, he wouldn't open the door. I heard him talking to someone. Finally, when he let me in, it smelled strongly like alpha in there. And he had no books." He shot us a glare. "He said he had fallen asleep and denied everything else, but when I went to meet my friends later, they said that the human alpha had been seen entering the same room as Latif and then escaping from the window later."

He rubbed his arm, looking wounded.

"I didn't know that omegas..." He fell silent, unable to say it, and my heart actually went out to him a little, despite the situation.

"It is a well-kept secret," Alya said gently. "I'm sure you understand. Omegas must be kept safe at all costs."

"Why?" Addy demanded. "They clearly *want* it."

"Addy!" his al-mother snapped. "That's enough."

He began to argue, but his al-mother stood.

"You've said your piece. Go wait outside."

He stared for a moment, then grit his teeth and pushed to his feet, marching angrily out the door.

"There is more," Latif's om-father said quietly. "I had falsely believed that the human Blaine would be safe around Latif. He promised to convince him to do an auction and Latif also agreed if he could go back to his training with Devin... I was fooled into believing them."

Latif's al-mother put an arm around his shoulders, comfortingly.

"Don't blame yourself," she said softly. "You did not know."

Suddenly, the front curtain flew open, and to my chagrin, *Alex* entered.

He lumbered into the room, gasping and sweating, and I was on my feet, ready to help him before Saar came rushing in after him, looking cross.

Alex pointed at me, then tried to say something but was too out of breath.

Saar quickly pulled out a chair, helping Alex into it.

"He should not be running around right now!" Saar admonished, glaring at me.

I stared.

"I didn't do anything!"

"You truly think that *Alex* would remain at home

upon hearing that you took advantage of an innocent nassa omega?" he demanded.

Eisa had just arrived and for some reason, he only nodded knowingly as he took his seat.

"After the lies he told to remove Alex from the planet in the first place, I am not surprised by any of this," he said.

"Don't act all high and mighty," Alex said, finally finding his voice. "You took an omega into the jungle for days! There were search parties!"

"Yes, but—" Eisa fell silent, thinking.

"Blaine, what the hell?!" Alex demanded. "I defended you!"

I winced but didn't move.

I was still standing, hands braced not the table, and everyone was right here.

"Latif is an adult," I said firmly. "I didn't coerce him. He *wanted* to do it because he doesn't want to get bonded to anyone. He just wanted some life experience."

I let that sink in while I tried to find words for the rest.

"Can you blame him?" I asked. "He is stuck in his house. He has no freedom whatsoever... Alex, none of the unmated omegas do. Please. Be honest with yourself. Are you really okay with that?"

He stared at me, his expressive eyes filled with conflict.

"It's their culture," he said weakly.

"It's about to be your child's culture too."

His face fell.

"Enough of this," Saar said, glaring at me. "You cannot come to our planet and try to change things."

"I'm not the one trying to change things," I said firmly. "Latif is. And I imagine that he's not the only unmated omega who is unhappy here."

A silence filled the room.

"We still cannot permit this type of behavior," Kion said, his voice firm. "I will arrange for your removal from Mukhana at once."

I nodded, readying myself for what was to come.

"I will be taking Alex with me."

Saar was on his feet at once, as were a few of the other alphas, but he was the only one who lunged for me.

I just managed to move out of his reach, nearly tripping into Latif's lap.

He steadied me as the others held Saar back.

Even Alex had stood.

"Blaine," he said, his voice full of exasperation, "what are you talking about?"

"You never told me about the poison kisses," I accused. "And I noticed it's conveniently absent from your essay about the bonding ceremonies. Once I report this, you're not going to be allowed to stay here. It's one thing for you to *want* to be here of your own free will, but—"

"You conniving bastard!" Saar shouted.

He jumped for me again, and this time, his claws scraped my shirt, slicing it open with ease before he was dragged from the room.

Alex stared at me, then looked back to the door Saar had been dragged through.

"We'll talk later," he said firmly, then went after his mate.

I stood there, chest heaving.

"You threaten my friend, you threaten me," Eisa informed me.

"You're lucky I'm not bringing Devin into this," I informed him. From what I understood, he had wanted to be here even before the bonding. Still... it felt wrong to leave any humans behind in this place. I was going to get it marked with a great big *omit* when I got out of here.

A growl filled the room, Eisa's chest reverberating with it.

"If you cannot remain calm, you may also go wait outside," Alpha Kion told him.

He remained where he was for a moment, angry green eyes fixed on me as though contemplating how quickly he could behead me.

Finally, he stood and went after Saar and Alex.

"You realize that you cannot forcibly take one of our people, don't you?" Alya asked. "Alex is ours. We will fight for him."

The other council members nodded their agreement.

I shook my head.

"I won't leave him here again," I said firmly. "The last time nearly killed me."

Silence filled the room once more. Then, Latif's hesitant voice.

"Alex?" he asked, sounding small.

I looked down at him. His exotic cobalt eyes were so filled with uncertainty, those lips I'd never even gotten to kiss turned down in a frown.

"But he's *pregnant*. You can't just... why *Alex*?"

For far too long, I stared down at Latif, unsure of what to say or how to explain. And fuck me. He was right. How the hell was I supposed to take Alex and leave *him* here?

I couldn't do it.

fourteen

. . .

LATIF

The distressed look in Blaine's eyes burned into me. He watched me for so long that, eventually, two of the council members came around the table to take him away. Still, he kept watching me, even turning to look at me over the shoulder as he was led from the building.

"Latif," Al-mother said gently. "It is time to go."

I started, turning to look at my parents. I had been staring unseeing at the door he had been taken through.

The others were gone. Whatever last words had been said, I hadn't heard them. In fact, nothing had truly registered after Blaine had said he wanted Alex to go with him.

I felt strange. Like I had left my body. Yet somehow I stood; I allowed myself to be directed out the door.

"There you are," Addy snapped. His tail thumped the ground in irritation, sending dust up around us. "I'm surprised you didn't go chasing after your little *human*."

I heard the disdain in his voice, but it didn't penetrate me the way it usually would.

"Not now," Om-father hissed.

He grumbled most of the way home and then made some declaration about being angry and that he would be home later. I didn't know. I barely heard him.

Al-mother and Om-father didn't say anything until we got home.

"Are you okay?" Al-mother asked.

I shook my head, then nodded, unsure.

"Do you need anything?" Om-father asked.

I shook my head again and went to my room.

It wasn't until I was in my bed, wrapped up in the blankets, that it all hit me.

I had wanted to rebel, to feel the intimacy that I never would. It had all been my idea.

I'd given Blaine all of me, hadn't I? And he had

only wanted Alex. He could have taken me away from here, but he didn't even think of it.

He had been kind and gentle with me. I had wanted him, and he had given me everything I asked for. This was all my fault and, yet, it *hurt*.

Quiet, dry sobs tore from my body. I pressed my face into a pillow to silence them.

Why had I been so stupid? I'd thought the library was safe. I hadn't accounted for how loud we would be, or how many people would be around us, close enough to hear. Meanwhile, I had been worried in the cave about visitors wandering in, but it had been so much better there.

If we had been smart, we could have kept seeing each other.

And what good would that be? I wondered. When Blaine had made it quite clear that all he cared about was Alex? Even though he was already taken.

I was here and I was free and yet—

I swallowed, realizing where my thoughts were taking me.

Did I want to bond with Blaine?

My eyes shot open, gaze flying to the tawny ceiling.

I had been rebelling so hard against what my parents wanted... Perhaps I had been blind to what *I* wanted, because it was the same thing.

I had never felt so humbled in my life as in that moment.

I *wasn't* special, was I?

No. I was completely typical. Omegas were kept apart, our secrets hidden so that we would not be swayed by alpha pheromones, and they would not be tempted by ours.

Then, the first time I'd been alone with an alpha, I had immediately acted on those urges.

If I had been strong, I would not have cared that Blaine was an alpha. I would not have wanted him so desperately. I would not still want him now, even after the humiliation he had made me feel sitting at his side while he said he wanted someone else.

I was so pathetic.

And worst of all, my parents were right about everything.

———

No one came to check on me. Perhaps they were worried about setting me off. Or maybe they were still angry. They had every right to be.

Sometime in the middle of the night, I heard Addy's belligerent voice shouting and then Al-mother putting him in his place, but I did not go check on them. I remained where I had fallen in bed hours ago, sick with sadness.

When the morning sun lifted above the horizon and the sky began to lighten, I was already awake, staring at the wall.

I heard the movements of the morning, Al-mother rising and readying herself for work on the boats and Om-father packing a meal.

They were talking quietly. I couldn't hear what they were saying, but I had the feeling that it was about me.

Sure enough, a few minutes later, my curtain parted, and Om-father entered tentatively with a tray of food.

"You did not eat last night," he said gently and then stood for a moment watching me.

"Oh, Latif," he sighed. "I'm so sorry you are going through this."

He set the tray down on the table and came to me, taking a seat next to me on the edge of the bed. He rubbed my back for a minute.

"I'm so sorry I put you in this position," he said sadly, but I shook my head.

"It wasn't you, Om-father," I whispered. "It was me. I'm so stupid."

He shook his head, frowning.

"Please don't say that."

"I am," I insisted. "Blaine was nice. He *was* trust-worthy. He wouldn't have touched me if I didn't insist."

Om-father looked away, biting his lip.

That must have been where I got that habit. Of course, all I could think about was how it drove Blaine crazy and just how much I had loved that.

"It is our nature to want to be intimate with some-one," Om-father finally said. "That doesn't make you stupid. Everyone wants love."

I snorted.

"I thought I was so *different*, but I'm just like everyone else."

"There is nothing wrong with being an omega," Om-father said, his voice firm. "Unless you think there is something wrong with me too."

I looked at him, surprised, but shook my head.

"No, Om-father," I said.

He smiled sadly.

"I am sorry I pushed you for the auctions," he admitted. "In the end, it is your choice. I just thought, instead of being stuck with us, you would prefer to be stuck with your soulmate."

Patting me on the shoulder, he stood.

"Please eat something," he said. "And when you feel like getting up, perhaps we could go to the healing pools or the temple."

I nodded, even though the idea of facing Naz's disappointment made my skin crawl.

Instead, I stayed just where I was, staring at the walls, Om-father's words resonating through me.

I wondered if he had ever said his argument quite like that before, or if I had simply been too hard-headed to hear it.

To simply switch my keeper to someone I did not yet know had seemed like a nightmare before. Now though, all I could think of was how quickly I had wanted Blaine.

I closed my eyes tightly.

Would I really feel the same way with someone else?

My thoughts and emotions spiraled all day. I did not know where Blaine was or what had happened to him. I did not know what decision had been made. I was in turmoil, yet I could not stop thinking about our times together. They had felt special.

Right from the moment Blaine had walked onto that field, I had been drawn to him. What had made me fight him that day?

And it was so strange: Devin's father was an unmated alpha, yet when he watched from the stands, no one minded. Was it because he was weak and unable to walk? That was the only answer I could think of.

If only we could have found a way to keep going in silence, to keep seeing each other forever where no one could have caught us.

It was such a silly dream that it almost made me laugh. As if no one would ever grow suspicious of us both spending so much time in the caves.

My swirling thoughts were driving me crazy, but they kept coming back to the same point. Over and over, I was led to one answer.

When I heard Al-mother's voice again from the living room, I finally dragged my body from bed. I hadn't remembered to eat, so I left the food where it was and stepped out of my room.

I walked down the hall in trepidation, their conversation growing louder. Just Om-father asking how her day had been. They were my parents, so I shouldn't have been scared, but my stomach swooped with fear over what I planned to do.

"How is Latif?" Al-mother asked just as I reached the doorway, but then she saw me standing there and froze.

"Hi," I muttered.

They both looked at me with such worry that for a moment I could not move.

"Come," Al-mother finally said. She came forward and ushered me onto one of the pouffes, taking a seat in front of me.

"Do you need anything?"

I swallowed.

"I want to talk to you both."

Remembering my brother's existence, I glanced around.

"Where is Addy?"

"He's on a rampage somewhere with his friends," Om-father said.

"He's mad at me," I guessed.

"No, he's mad that no one is punishing you. He doesn't understand what you are going through."

I nodded at Al-mother's words then pushed my thoughts to the matter at hand.

"I'm sorry that I've been so difficult lately."

They both began to argue, and I couldn't help a small smile.

"It is okay, you don't have to lie for the sake of my feelings."

At that, they fell silent, both looking somber.

"And I know that everyone in the whole city probably knows what happened, but," I took a trembling breath, squeezing my shaking hands into fists, "if any alpha still wants me..."

I had to force the last words out.

"I will have an auction."

A silence followed my words, until I finally chanced a glance up at them.

Neither of them looked as overjoyed as I'd thought they would.

"I think that would be for the best," Al-mother finally said, voice gentler than I had ever heard it.

Om-father gave me a big hug and didn't let go.

"You will be so happy," he whispered into my hair. "Trust me. Everything will be just fine."

His words made my stomach ache.

"Tomorrow?" Al-mother asked.

Om-father nodded.

"The sooner, the better. It does not take long to spread the word."

Om-father finally smiled.

"I will tell the alpha council the good news," she said.

I managed a nod.

"Will we pick your auction robes together in the morning?" Om-father asked, excitement tinting his voice.

I managed a nod even though the thought already exhausted me.

"Who will we have on the podium with us?" Om-father asked.

They fell into a discussion about what was to come. But it was becoming a habit for me to hear nothing but my own thoughts.

"Can I go back to bed now?" I asked.

After a long moment, they both nodded.

I retreated to my room, back into the same cocoon of blankets I'd been hiding myself in all day.

I'd said the words. It was happening now, and I wouldn't back down.

After all, I had nothing left to lose.

fifteen

. . .

BLAINE

The cell I'd been locked in was nowhere near as welcoming as my house had been. It turned out that the nassa had doors for two things: keeping omegas safe and keeping prisoners.

So much for the utopia Alex had painted.

They hadn't even let me talk to my human higher-ups. Not with the threat I'd given about taking Alex with me.

I felt conflicted thinking about it now though. Since the heat of the moment had passed and I'd had the pleasure of nothing but my overbearing thoughts as company, my threat just felt *wrong*.

Alex was pregnant and he insisted that he was happy here. Was tearing apart their family truly the answer? Then there was the little issue of Saar *dying* if they were apart.

I may have forgotten that little tidbit.

So, yeah, I could take Alex away, but he would absolutely hate me for it.

And anyway, that wasn't the thing that bothered me the most.

I didn't think I would ever forgive myself for the way that Latif had looked at me yesterday. I'd let them take me away, because how was I supposed to fight it? But I felt like I'd left him in a den of wolves. The other nassa didn't understand him the way that I did. They cared about him maybe, but he needed more than that.

He needed *me*.

They wouldn't let me take him away. I knew that much. But the idea of leaving him behind was eating me up inside.

If only I could find a way to stay...

Voices suddenly carried through the air toward me.

Curious, I went to the window and peered down. It wasn't barred, but there was a steep drop to the ground from up here and guards relaxing down there. And to my surprise, Alex stood there, talking to them for a moment, before continuing inside.

I took a breath, readying myself for his arrival.

When Alex did enter, key in hand and everything, I simply shook my head.

"They are far too trusting here," I said. "How do they know I'm not going to shove you over and run away?"

Alex grinned but took a moment to rest his hands on his belly and breathe.

"Well," he panted, "they would probably stop you at the door."

"Ah. Right."

He smiled, then suddenly looked around the room with wide eyes.

"Hey, this was where I was kept on my first night here!" he enthused.

Immediately, he went to the window and stuck his head outside, looking down, chuckling.

"I didn't realize it was the same two guards too. Nice guys. Hello down there!"

"Hello Alex!" someone shouted from below.

I frowned.

"This is the strangest imprisonment I've ever experienced."

Alex looked back at me.

"You've been imprisoned before?" he asked.

I shrugged, not offering any info. After the cover-up job on Lycea, I'd had to keep it to myself all these years, so it was second nature now.

Sighing, Alex came to the bed, where I was sitting and took a seat next to me.

"I wanted to talk to you," he said.

"To convince me to keep my mouth shut about the poison?"

"They call it poison," Alex said, "just like they call the fights an auction. It's not quite the language we would use."

"What do you mean?"

He shrugged lightly.

"It's an aphrodisiac. It makes you horny for a bit."

"For the specific person who kissed you," I argued.

"Exactly," Alex argued. "I'd already kissed Saar. I'd gone along with it all."

"To save yourself."

"Well, yeah, that's true. But I *was* into him already. And wanting to stay here came after that."

I knew I should drop it now. It was hard though because—well, because of everything else.

"I don't want you to be unhappy," I finally said. "It's not that."

"Then what is it?"

I froze for a moment, wondering how to explain,

and then, because this was Alex and I trusted him, I let it all fall out.

"Years ago, I had a first contact mission on Lycea," I said. The planet's name sounded heavy falling from my lips.

"Almost the entire place is under water, their people are all sea dwellers. Octopi and mer, and they are extremely fierce. It was shortly after my first promotion and things were going well with them, but one of my underlings made a blunder. He said something he shouldn't have. A stupid joke about humans being a force to reckon with."

I paused, memories flashing.

"What happened?" Alex asked gently.

"They executed him," I said. "Right on the spot."

"Shit," Alex muttered.

"Yeah," I breathed, trying to come back to the moment. "No warning. And he was young too. But we'd known to be careful with them and no one wanted to start another war, so we pretended it was an accident and marked the planet *omit*. It was my fault as much as it was his. I should have warned him. No one else thought so though."

Alex shook his head.

"It wasn't. You can't control what someone is going to say. You couldn't make me walk back to the pods that day. I wanted to leave our security behind."

"I know," I groaned. "And I know this isn't Lycea. I know you like it here, but I just can't stop feeling like it's the same thing. You trusted me and I brought you here. And I left you here."

"Then you did and said just the right thing to get me back," Alex reminded me. "You did that, Blaine. You pretended to be my mate. You faced Saar and he *hates* you, no offense. You even came here again just to help me with my research and... shit. Now I have a confession."

I frowned.

"What is it?" I asked. "Because I don't think I can handle any bad news right now."

He pursed his lips.

"I know my research could have waited for me," he finally admitted. "I just wanted my friend to come visit."

I stared, jaw dropping.

"Alex," I said slowly. "Do you have any idea how expensive this *visit* is for HFC?"

He pouted.

"Yeah, but I'm pregnant and I *missed* you."

Suddenly, I couldn't stop laughing.

Alex started to crack up next to me too, but the party ended when the door suddenly opened, revealing Saar on the other side, looking like a kicked puppy.

"Alex," he said sternly, "you are going to be the death of me."

Before he could argue, Saar stalked into the room.

"First, you sneak away, making me worry. Then, you come here to visit the very man planning on stealing you away again. And now I learn that you lied to get him to visit you?"

Alex grimaced.

"You heard that, huh?"

He sighed heavily.

"I heard *all* of it. The whole conversation."

Looking tired, he flopped down onto the bed on my other side.

For the first time since my arrival here, Saar didn't look like he wanted to kill me.

I offered a smile, but he did not return it.

"Blaine," he said instead, "I believe you are no longer planning to take my mate away?"

I nodded resolutely.

"That would be correct. He's all yours."

Sighing, he patted me on the back.

"Of course, this does not excuse your actions with Latif," he added.

"Maybe."

I swallowed, eyeing Saar.

If anyone knew about the council's goings on, it would be one of its members.

"Has my pickup already been arranged?" I asked tentatively.

"Not as of yet," Saar admitted. "We have been busy arranging—"

He paused, and he and Alex exchanged a look.

"What is it?" I asked.

"Latif is having an auction," Alex finally said.

They both watched my reaction carefully.

It took a moment for that to hit me.

"Today?" I asked.

They both nodded.

"That can't be right," I argued. Then I realized it most certainly could. His family had cared about that more than anything.

"No. You have to stop it."

Again, they exchanged that look.

"See, I told you he wasn't like that," Alex said smugly.

"What?" I demanded.

"I told Saar that you wouldn't have slept with Latif unless you actually cared for him."

I didn't know what to say to that.

"*Of course* I care for him!"

I stood, pacing the small room. His expression in those last moments plagued me.

"And I *know* him. He would never enter these auctions of his own free will. He doesn't *want* to be bound to some alpha."

"It will not be *some alpha*," Saar argued. "It will be his fated mate."

That made me pause.

I spun around to face them.

"What do you mean?"

"That you need not worry about him. Fate decides the winner. No matter what, his soulmate will win."

My heart pounded in my chest.

"No matter what?" I repeated. "What if it's me?"

Saar seemed to like that idea because a fire lit his eyes.

"You wish to compete?"

"*No*, Blaine. They're massive, *weaponized*, aliens."

"If he wants to fight, he *should*. You know better than us, Blaine. Follow your instincts."

"He doesn't know how to fight the way that you all do," Alex argued.

"It does not matter," Saar argued back. "The right mate always wins."

"I'm better suited to be with Latif than any other alpha on this planet. I know that."

It was weird to feel so sure about something like this, but it was like everything was suddenly clicking into place. Latif needed an alpha to win him. To have the freedom that he wanted, *I* was that alpha. If I entered that competition and anyone other than me was left standing, then there was no such thing as fate. If there was such a thing, it had already brought us together more than once, and it was doing so again right now.

"It won't prove anything," Alex said, worried. "You'll just get beat up and they'll still think whoever wins is his soulmate."

Saar stiffened, his gaze shooting to Alex.

"It's not that I don't think we're meant to be together," he groaned. "We are. I have no doubt of that. I just don't want to see Blaine get hurt. He's not a nassa warrior."

But now, unexpectedly, Saar was the one who had my back.

"It does not matter," he insisted again. "If Blaine means what he is saying, then he *will* win."

With that, he turned, meeting my sure gaze.

"I will take you there."

sixteen

. . .

LATIF

It was strange to be in such an upbeat, happy atmosphere while I felt like I was dying inside.

I didn't even regret that I had decided to do this. It was just that I felt numb inside. There was a common balm that could be used on bruises and cuts to numb the area while it healed. I imagined it was something like that.

When I was ready to open my heart again, Blaine wouldn't even have left a scar behind.

For the sake of Om-father, I smiled while we picked my clothing.

He thought a shimmery blue would be nice to

draw out the color of my scales, and I agreed. He suggested that the sandals we chose should be clean and white. With the desert sand, we so rarely wore white, so I thought that was a nice idea too.

After that, a large group of friends met to get ready. Almost everyone from my classes came. To my surprise, both Devin and Alex joined.

Devin greeted me with a hug, patting my back with that warm smile he had.

"Excited?" he asked.

I forced a nod.

"Yes. My parents are very pleased."

"Your parents?" Alex interjected. "Not you?"

He seemed to be trying to read me, his pale blue eyes searching my face with rapt attention.

I shrugged helplessly.

"Of course, I am happy too," I lied weakly. "Why wouldn't I be?"

He searched my eyes a moment longer and then a soft smile touched his lips.

"Okay," he said, patting my arm. "*Good.*"

He passed me then to greet the others, but Devin lingered, shooting Alex a curious look.

"Not to pry, but you seem pretty upset about this," he said. "Is there any way you can get out of it?"

I frowned.

"Is it that obvious?" I asked quietly.

He grimaced, patting my arm.

"Is it about Blaine?" he asked, then winced. "I know I probably shouldn't bring it up. I heard what happened."

I laughed humorlessly.

"Everyone did," I said. "I'll be lucky if anyone arrives to fight for me. I'm lucky anyone even came to celebrate with me now."

Devin pursed his lips.

"Hey, don't brush us off so quickly," he admonished. "You know I was in the same position as you for my auction. Me and Eisa were alone for days in the jungle. We even bonded."

I stared at Devin. Why hadn't I come to him sooner?

He gave me an amused look, brows raised. "Crazy, right?"

I managed a nod while my thoughts raced, questions jumbling together.

"What was it like?" I finally asked.

Devin winced.

"Breaking the bond first, that sucked. But Eisa wanted to win me the 'proper way' and there was nothing I could do to change his mind."

He made a funny movement with the first two fingers on both hands, like he was scratching the air, but I would not let his human tics distract me while we were speaking about something so important.

"I remember hearing about it," I admitted. "To be honest, I thought you had been taken and bonded against your will at first, so I was worried for you."

He patted my arm, smiling.

"I know. Everyone thought that until we cleared it all up."

"And then Eisa won you back," I said.

"Yes, with a little help from me." He winked.

I frowned.

"What do you mean?" I asked slowly.

"I instructed him through the fight," he said, smiling fondly at the memory. "I knew that nassa didn't know how to fight the way that I did, and Eisa listened. We beat those alphas together."

Once again, I was left dumbstruck.

"Is that allowed?" I asked slowly.

He shrugged.

"I guess so. No one complained." He grinned and leaned closer to whisper. "I wasn't about to let anyone but Eisa get me."

I had only heard that Eisa had won. Then again, hadn't Addy been particularly disgruntled after returning from that event?

I seemed to recall Al-mother telling him to "accept it and be quiet."

Devin patted my arm once more and moved past me to talk to the others.

I turned around and looked at them all.

Most of them were mated, of course, aside from some friends who would not be coming to the pit with us. Alil caught my eye at once and came over, hugging me.

"You look so nervous," he said. "Come to the water and relax for a bit."

I allowed myself to be led to the hot pool and took a spot among my friends. It was easier in the group to remember that I was supposed to be happy and excited. I almost fell for it, slowly feeling my mood lift.

Om-father sat behind me, taking great care in braiding my hair while we all chatted.

Eventually, he placed a quick kiss to the top of my hair and released me.

"There. All done," he said, sounding nervous himself. "And it is almost time to go."

I looked back at Om-father, all the nerves rushing straight back into me. Everyone else was smiling encouragingly but I felt like I was going to be sick.

I climbed out and dried myself, then carefully pulled all the new fabric onto my body. To my surprise, Om-father used his own belt to tie it on, smiling at me.

I looked down at the thick golden rope, studded with blue and orange jewels. He always wore this one on special occasions.

Suddenly, my hands started shaking. Everything felt too real.

"I can't do this," I whispered.

He took my hands, squeezing them tightly.

"Latif, please believe me. Whatever you felt for Blaine, you will be feeling again. And it will be right this time."

I shut my eyes, aware that the others were gathering around us. Those who were joining us at the auction were already dressed up and ready to go.

Taking a trembling breath, I nodded.

"Okay, let's go."

We began to walk together. To keep my appearance a surprise, I was blocked from all angles by veils that danced against the wind.

Finally, we reached the tall wall to the pit and the ladder that led directly onto the pew.

I could hear a crowd. They were so loud even from out here, it made me even more nervous to reveal myself. Almost the whole of Diwan was here to see me and my bond-mate-to-be...

We began to climb, one by one. When it was Alex's turn, he was given a hand, but I had never seen him look so nervous.

I followed him up.

As I stepped out onto the pew, the huge crowd erupted into noise. For a moment, I stood there, shocked by the number of people, all in one place.

I had never entered the pit before, and descriptions didn't prepare me for the real experience. The energy in the air, the fighting pit below, and the prestigious position above everyone, dressed up with the alpha council at my side as though I was one of them.

It was humbling.

Devin caught my attention, waving me over.

As Eisa and Saar were part of the alpha council, they were both here. The others took seats around us. I sat next to Om-father, and a moment later Al-mother arrived with Addy, taking the seats next to us.

Addy glanced at me and nodded, but he looked like he hadn't been sleeping and wasn't very happy. Al-mother, on the other hand, smiled so happily at me that I couldn't help returning it even though I was trembling.

We had also invited a few family friends to join us —Alil's parents being some of them, which just made me sad he couldn't have joined us too. I needed as many friends as I could have right now.

At least Devin was here.

I caught sight of Alex a few seats over and was

surprised to see that he still looked nervous. He was fidgeting so much that Saar eventually took his hand and bent to whisper in his ear.

I assumed he was trying to calm him, but Alex only squeezed his eyes shut and shook his head, looking even more scared.

Cold traveled down my spine, even on this hot afternoon. I knew suddenly that something was going to happen, but I didn't know what.

Head Alpha Kion stood, beginning to talk into his speaker, announcing me.

I smiled when everyone cheered but my stomach felt like lead.

I could not just sit here, so I leaned over Om-father, inclining far enough over that I could catch Alex's eyes even past Devin and Eisa.

"Alex," I hissed, and my voice came out harder than I meant it to. "What is happening?"

His worried gaze shot to me.

"Nothing," he whispered.

"Then why do you look so scared?" I demanded.

Om-father nudged me, trying to remind me of where I was, but Blaine's name was repeating in my head. Had something happened to him?

Alex bit his lip, exchanging a glance with Saar who shrugged helplessly.

"It's just... It's because of Blaine," he finally admitted, sagging.

My heart raced.

"What?" I demanded. "What has happened to him? Please!"

"No, nothing has happened to him," he insisted. "*Yet.*"

"Now bring in the alphas!" Head Alpha Kion bellowed.

The crowd erupted, but I couldn't tear my eyes from Alex's face to see who had come to try to win me.

"Where is he?"

Alex, grimaced, meeting my gaze apologetically before pointing *into the pit.*

No.

I turned, shock reverberating through me.

There were more alphas than I'd expected but I didn't have the time to count them all, because my eyes were fixed on the one person that mattered. The human amongst them. The one who had made me feel seen and wanted and respected. The one who was willing to risk it all to be with me. The one who *didn't know how to fight.*

Panic and absolute elation lifted me to my feet.

"Oh!" Om-father exclaimed behind me. "He has to win!"

I couldn't agree more.

The desire to laugh and scream at the same time warred within me, leaving me standing there, stunned, my hands on the railings, unable to do anything but watch.

That was, until the alphas began to move toward one another and I saw them approaching Blaine.

Devin's words about the rules rang in my ears. All my life, I had heard about fate intervening to pick the auction winners. That meant that everything I did was meant to be, did it not?

Without thinking, I cleared the railing.

I landed in the pit in my sparkling jewels, getting my white sandals dirty at once as it all became clear.

I'd wanted to fight for myself. I'd wanted to make my own choices. I wanted to show I was as strong as any alpha.

Well, now I was about to.

There was shouting behind me. I could hear Al-mother's frantic voice and Devin's cheering. The crowd was deafening but as I stood to my full height, all sound faded into a rush of white noise.

The alphas hadn't noticed me yet. That didn't matter. Just this once, I did not mind playing dirty. The two nearest me were facing off, oblivious to what was happening.

I rushed one of them, tackling him with my full strength.

The takedown was too easy. I'd thought alphas would be harder to defeat than omegas were, but I would bet that every omega in my class could have done this easily.

He struggled for a moment, unable to see who had bested him, but I expertly maneuvered him into a headlock until he flailed wildly, his face turning purple.

Oh, I'd forgotten they didn't know how to tap.

I released him.

"Off the field," I ordered, pleased. "One down."

I spun, finding the other alpha that had been there standing still, staring at me in shock.

As though unable to believe his eyes, he looked up at the podium, then back to me.

When I moved toward him, he hastily readied himself for an attack, but it didn't matter. There was no one here that I could not defend myself against, and finally, everyone would know it.

seventeen

. . .

BLAINE

Latif was a force to be reckoned with, and not just because he went through every alpha on the field like a warm knife through butter.

A strange calmness had fallen over me when the doors had been opened into the arena, and now I knew why.

Saar was right. No matter what, I was going to be the last one standing. Latif was seeing to that himself and I'd never been so freaking proud in my life.

All around me, huge nassa warriors were struggling back up to their feet while Latif bent their bodies this way and that with such ease that it was almost ridiculous.

Finally, one other alpha remained.

Latif faced him, *grinning*, and I couldn't help but laugh, because he was enjoying this far too much.

The alpha, seeing the look on Latif's face, raised his hands in surrender and backed toward the sidelines.

Still grinning, Latif turned, facing me for the first time. He was in a dirty blue gown and had mud on his cheek. His hair was a fuzzy mess with flyaways everywhere, bright blue in the sunlight. He had never looked so beautiful.

Chest heaving, he marched over to me, not stopping until we collided.

His arms came around me, crushing me to his chest, and I met the embrace with equal enthusiasm.

Suddenly, he pulled back.

"You said you were going to take *Alex* away with you," he said, frowning. "And not me."

I shook my head, unable to stop smiling.

"I was an utter idiot," I said. "And anyway, I thought you wanted to stay here and change things."

I stepped forward, taking his hands in mine.

"Latif," I said, warmly, "I think you just did."

He froze for a moment and his gaze flew past me as though finally seeing the crowd beyond. They were shockingly quiet now, all eyes on us. Emotion filled his eyes, and he took a shaking breath, squeezing my hands in his.

"Do you really want to stay here with me?" he asked, voice shaking.

"I was willing to die for the chance to."

He met my eyes again, his gaze fierce.

"Good thing I didn't let you."

With that, he turned, facing the podium.

"Blaine is the last alpha standing!" he shouted, chin raised, as though that was that. Just in case anyone argued.

Head Alpha Kion rose, speaker in hand.

"Interesting," he said into it. I could see that he was smiling from here. "The human alpha Blaine is the winner!"

I reached out, taking Latif's hand in mine and squeezing it. I hadn't put two and two together. That us bonding would fix the other things—the things we'd done. I was reminded of a shotgun wedding, but when we were lifted onto a thrown and carried through the streets, and the whole city celebrated for us, I suddenly understood Mukhana and the nassa a little bit more.

They valued unity and love above all else. How could I complain about that? And by going along with what they wanted, to a degree, we had gotten what we wanted too.

I leaned toward Latif, laughing when the swaying throne knocked me into his shoulder a little too hard.

"What you did back there was amazing."

"When I saw you there, it was like I came alive," Latif said, smiling at me.

My entire body buzzed with excitement for what was to come. Not just right now on Mount Ethos but for our future together.

The party lasted all the way to the base of the mountain. The staircase that Alex had described was narrower than I expected. I guessed that was why there was a procession to get up to the top.

As the throne was lowered to the ground, Devin reached us.

He pulled Latif into a big bear hug, squeezing him tightly.

"I guess you really do listen in class," he joked, finally pulling back.

Latif grinned.

"Sometimes," he agreed.

Two familiar faces suddenly appeared to greet us. I couldn't help but grimace a little at the sight of Latif's parents. Last time I'd seen them, they'd pretty much wanted to kill me.

"Um, hello," I said and was promptly pulled into a hug by his om-father.

He squeezed me tightly.

"I suppose I was right about you the first time. Only a good alpha would risk himself like that for my son."

"He's worth it," I said, smiling. "And thanks to him, I didn't even get a scratch."

"Yes," his al-mother agreed. "That was very impressive, Latif... I suppose I should have given your training more credit."

Latif beamed.

"I tried to tell you."

He looked around then, searching the crowd.

"Where is Addy?"

"We lost him somewhere in the crowd after leaving the pit," Om-father said. "I'm sure he'll show up by the time we're at the top."

"Shall we?" Al-mother asked, patting my shoulder and directing us toward the mountain.

The marching band was already in line and the alpha council seemed to be ready to begin, all their mates in tow.

But I caught sight of Alex among them and frowned.

"Hang on," I muttered.

Still holding Latif's hand in my own, I went to where Alex and Saar were standing, quietly talking.

"You should stay down here," I said by way of greeting.

Alex squeezed his eyes tightly shut.

"Ugh. Why do you sound like Saar again?"

"Because he is an alpha and he sees reason," Saar said. "You don't look well."

Alex pouted.

"I can't believe I'm about to say this, but you're both right. I don't know if I can make it up there."

"What is wrong?" Latif asked.

"Cramps," Alex gasped. "And the baby is doing something crazy."

He winced and tears filled his eyes.

Saar's parents had arrived and frowned down at his belly.

"I must go to the top to officiate the bond," Head Alpha Kion said. "But you two remain here. Go home and call the medic."

Saar nodded resolutely but, before going anywhere, turned to me.

"You showed great strength in entering the pit against fifteen nassa alphas," he said. "For that alone, I wish you and Latif everything you desire."

He reached out, offering me his hand in a very human fashion that he must have learned from Alex.

I took it, a lightness filling me at the strange thought that, somehow, this alien that I'd hated might end up being a friend.

Then he smiled at Latif.

"And you may have shaken our very society today," he said.

Latif shook his head bashfully, looking incredibly pleased.

"So inspiring!" Alex agreed and then gasped again, his hand flying to his lower stomach.

With that, Saar bent, scooping him up in his arms and bidding us farewell.

The climb up the mountain was surprisingly enjoyable. The air got cooler, the drums played out a beat that made it easier to climb to, and the higher we got, the more incredible the view.

As we cleared the peak, Latif swung around to face me, grinning.

"To be honest," he said, "I always wanted to see this place, but I never thought I would be able to."

The building up here was high enough to be in the clouds if not for the clear sky. It almost reminded me of Mount Olympus. It must have been old. I wondered if it was from the time of the cave drawings and just as expertly maintained.

Taking Latif's hand, I pulled him to the side where we could see all of Diwan far below us.

Standing behind him, I wrapped my arms around his waist. Resting my chin on his shoulder, I took in the breathtaking view. The city looked beautiful from up here. The whole planet did. Grudgingly, I had to admit it wasn't so bad here, and not just because of the sweet omega that was currently in my arms. It wasn't perfect, but if they would let Latif win at his own auction, maybe that meant things could change. It would be worth it for Latif and other omegas to talk to them about. But that was a discussion for another day. For now, this was all about *us*.

His loose strands of hair blew in the breeze and the sun through them reminded me.

"Oh."

Smiling, I pulled back, gently extracting the light catcher from my back pocket.

"I nearly forgot," I said, lifting it up, letting it hang by the chain. It really was incredible how close the color was to his eyes.

"I know it's not much, but this made me think of you. After that first day we met."

Latif's eyes widened.

He took it carefully from my hands, examining it like it was a fine gem.

"I will treasure it," he promised and apparently it wasn't a suncatcher after all, because he put the rope around his neck and hooked the end into the chain by the base. It hung perfectly like a necklace, the large pendant dangling in the center of his chest.

"Oh dear," his om-father said, seeming to come out of nowhere, "that is such a beautiful gift and yet the rest of you is such a mess."

He spent a minute frantically trying to pull Latif back together while we grinned at each other.

"Your hair is impossible," his om-father sighed.

Latif shrugged.

"Perhaps I can cut it short then," he suggested. "Like the humans do."

He was watching for my reaction.

"If you want," I said. "I'm sure you'll be able to pull it off."

They both tilted their heads in confusion at the expression.

"I just mean, you'll look good no matter what," I said.

"Oh yes," his om-father agreed wholeheartedly. "Latif is beautiful in anything."

"It's time to begin!" one of the council members called.

My heart started pounding, especially when I realized that me and Latif were meant to enter alone.

This was it. If I had any second thoughts, they should come out now. All I could think though was that I would finally get to feel those lips against my own.

I'd had no idea where to go next. I'd wanted to settle down somewhere, perhaps do remote classes. It was like everything I wanted but hadn't had the fortitude to arrange on my own was being pushed into my arms. Starting with Latif.

I hadn't set out to win him, yet as we walked into the cavernous room toward the alpha council, I was taken by the idea that fate had decided to intervene and, for whatever reason, give me everything.

We stopped before the alphas, still squeezing each other's hands tightly.

Kion stood, nodding to us.

"Blaine Human and Latif Nassia, we have gathered in this sacred place to bless your union and witness your consummation before the spirits and powers of the universe."

"Blaine, do you promise to love and protect your omega for the rest of your life?" Kion asked.

"Yes," I said.

There was no other answer.

"Latif, do you promise to love and support your alpha for the rest of your life?"

"Yes, I do," Latif promised.

"Then, with the alpha council as witness, you may consummate this bond."

We turned to face each other.

There had been no hesitation in Latif's voice and his gaze was just as sure when our eyes met, but I felt like I had to remind him.

"When we met, you didn't want this. You'll be stuck with me *forever*," I said. "It's not too late to back out now. I'll still love you, even if we aren't bound together."

His eyes widened.

"You love me?" he asked.

I shook my head and laughter huffed from between my lips.

"Isn't that obvious?"

Instead of answering, Latif stepped up against me, pressing his lips to mine.

He breathed into the kiss and my eyes squeezed shut, arms wrapping around him, wanting to pull him close enough that I never had to let go. His lips were softer than I'd thought they would be, and surer, and it lit a fire inside me, just like I'd been told it would. More than that though, it made everything as clear as polished glass. This was exactly where I was meant to be.

Eventually, he smiled against my lips.

"I love you too," he whispered.

eighteen

. . .

LATIF

It wasn't that Blaine's lips were *better* than the rest of him per se, but having his lips against mine, being able to kiss him at will, even in front of everyone else only reminded me of what was to come.

The crowd gathered around us, filling the room. The music was lively and fun. All the couples danced. But I just wanted to find a quiet spot with my new mate.

My new mate.

The thought made my heart race in the best of ways because Blaine was mine. And I was his. And it was all so very traditional and cliché, except for the fact that I had stood my ground and showed my strength in front of everyone, and Blaine had been alpha enough to stand back and let me and not be offended or have his ego hurt. His support for me moved me. We were the perfect match.

"I'm not much of a dancer," he said while we watched the couples move across the floor. "But I'll dance if you want to."

I almost said no, but then remembered that this was our bonding day and we should try to cherish it. Still, I could not help but want to simply run to our room together.

We went to the dance floor and *finally*, I was in his arms again.

Even though he said he could not dance, he swung me around a few times, making me move in an unexpected way that made my gown twirl around us.

Laughing, I allowed it until he pulled me in close at the start of a slower song and I clung to him, not wanting to part again.

The heat in his gaze was mingled with adoration now and I couldn't look at it without nerves shivering through me.

"Do you feel the poison?" I asked quietly, biting my lip.

He moaned softly and pressed his lips to mine,

pulling the soft flesh free with a swipe of the tongue that made me shiver.

"What do you think?" he asked quietly.

"Alright, go get a room! You really don't need to hang out here. We're fine."

We broke apart, chuckling at Devin's voice.

He and Eisa were next to us, dancing and watching knowingly.

Around us, everyone else was enjoying the party. Even Om-father and Al-mother were sitting together by one of the pillars, whispering while they gazed at each other lovingly. I supposed each person here was reminded of their own bond. They'd all had their day here. They all understood.

I looked at Blaine. He was watching me, waiting even though he was already hard where we were pressed together.

"Let's go," I said.

He didn't hesitate. Together, we practically ran from the dance floor.

Blaine pulled me into the hall, trying doors as we went. As the whole bonding temple was meant to be used for bonding and mating, they all had proper doors with locks.

Each one that he opened was a bedroom, but Blaine didn't pull me into the first one he found.

"Too small," he muttered, pulling the door shut again.

He tried a few more before finally pausing in the doorway of one of the rooms.

This one was bigger than the others and the bed was large with plenty of room.

My heart raced at the sight of it and instead of waiting for Blaine, I simply pushed him inside.

"I can't wait any longer," I said. "I need you inside me again."

He shuddered.

"Oh, god, I can't argue that."

He practically slammed the door behind us, sealing us in darkness and a moment later, I heard a lock click.

It was very dim in here. Only the smallest bit of light came in under the door. But even though I knew that Blaine could not see me, his hands found me at once, unceremoniously beginning to pull my belt off and tug my clothes.

I helped to take them off, shivering as the cool air hit my naked skin.

"Should we start the fire?" I asked.

He was ripping off his own clothes, shaking his head.

When he stepped up to me naked, we both shivered.

"We don't need a fire to warm up," he said, and pressed his lips to mine again.

It was a strange feeling in a way. Having our faces so close together, lips touching, but it was so nice too. His mouth was soft and inviting and it made me want to *enter* him somehow.

As though reading my thoughts and leading by example, he pressed his tongue between my lips.

For a moment, I was stunned. Then the sensation of his tongue against mine set my nerves alight *everywhere*. I clung to him, allowing him to sensually drag his tongue against mine, to touch the roof of my mouth, to explore, until I was rock hard and moaning softly.

When he pulled back, I could barely breathe and didn't care.

I followed, pressing my mouth to his for more, taking my turn to taste him the way that he had tasted me.

It was so intimate that even the sex we'd had before paled by comparison. What would it feel like to have him inside me, thrusting into my wet hole and my wet mouth at the same time?

I rutted against his hard length, bumping the wet tip while I started to drip from behind.

It was like my body knew what was to come and was extra eager this time because I didn't think I had ever been quite so slick without even being touched.

Blaine seemed to have a sixth sense for touching me the way I wanted. I was starting to think he could sense my pheromones in his own way, without realizing it, because he dropped his hand to my rear, feeling the slickness with his fingers.

He moaned, rubbing my hole until I was clenching and unable to help bucking back for more.

I finally broke our kiss, gasping and crying out as he pressed two fingers inside.

For a moment, I clung to him, pressing my face against his throat where it smelled the strongest and riding his fingers and then, suddenly, I realized that his hard length was against my thighs, waiting innocently. Without thinking, I lifted my leg, wrapping it around his waist.

He realized what I was doing at once and released his fingers, gripping his member instead to direct it where I wanted it.

I relaxed back, taking his length inside me, pacing myself as he stretched me open. My head fell back, a gasp on my lips as I took his full length.

"Oh," I gasped. "Finally."

"Yeah," he grunted, rocking his hips slowly back and forth. "Did you miss this?"

That was such an understatement that I wanted to

cry. I could not live without Blaine's thick length inside me, breaking me open into a panting, shaking mess.

He gripped me around the waist, keeping me upright, and I clung to his shoulders, loving the new sensation of doing this while standing and embracing. It felt so lovely. Each thrust seemed to undo me. I didn't want it to stop, but when I started to shake too hard, Blaine pulled his length free and pushed me gently back until I stumbled toward the bed.

"Lay back," he whispered sweetly. "Relax. Let me take care of you."

I groaned, falling onto the bedding, shivering all over again.

He climbed on after me, bracing his knees under my thighs, but instead of pushing straight back into me, he started to touch me everywhere, running his fingers and then his lips all over me.

When he bent and bit gently on my nipple, his fingers squeezing the other side, I bucked at the unexpected pleasure. He doubled down, sucking harder until my own length was dripping wet.

Humming in pleasure, he went there next, sucking my tip into his mouth, devouring the liquid that seeped from the tip while his fingers continued to play with the nubs of my nipples.

"I'm going to come," I gasped.

I sounded upset even to my own ears because the idea of finishing without Blaine impaling me was a devastating thought.

Maybe he knew that, because he lifted off suddenly, waiting a moment while my member flexed at the sudden loss.

Once I caught my breath, he slid his hips closer and gripped his length.

It was still wet from my slick, and I could hear it as he stroked up and down.

"Ready for more?" he asked.

I nodded, lifting my hips.

I was more than ready. I was desperate.

"I need you," I murmured.

He moaned.

"I will never get tired of hearing that," he promised.

He directed his tip to my hole again, rubbing it on the opening a few times, and then pressed inside, groaning.

I took a shuddering breath, and when he started to move, all sense of control left me. There was no need to hold back or be quiet. This was my mate. We were bonded. We were one.

I cried out, moving with a full sense of abandon, thrusting up to meet his hips. Slapping and the wet sounds of my slick filled the air as he pounded his length into me. Our moans and cries grew louder too, until finally I clenched around him, stars bursting in front of my eyes, pleasure overwhelming me.

His lips pressed to mine, tongue filling me as I came, and I knew nothing could top this moment except for *more*. And this time I could rest easy knowing I could have as much of this as I wanted from now on.

Blaine was mine as much as I was his.

nineteen

. . .

BLAINE

I wasn't eager to leave this little haven of ours.
Waking up in the cool, dark room tangled up with
Latif was heavenly.

And to be able to press kisses to his lips freely,
waking him with my touches, was even better. Before
I'd fully woken up, I had him on his back, legs
wrapped around my hips, rutting both our cocks
against each other until a whine left his throat.

"Inside," he begged, and I shuddered and
complied, pressing my hard cock into him. Before I
could move, his ankles tightened around my back
and he started to thrust up, squeezing my length up

and down, fucking himself on me until we both clung to each other helplessly as we came.

"Oh, fuck," I groaned, then tried to gently pry myself off him. "We have to stop this time, or we'll be going all day again."

Latif laughed breathlessly.

"I can't help myself," he admitted.

We lay on our backs next to each other until we could breathe.

Then, Latif sat up, looking around.

"I think there's a bath up here somewhere," he said. "Should we find it?"

We got dressed and began to search the building, only stumbling upon a few of the sleeping couples in our search.

When we finally found the room with the tub, it was secluded.

We climbed into the chilly water, washing up quickly. Then Latif turned, not so casually checking me out.

He bit his lip, staring at my cock.

"I can't believe I had that inside me. I can't believe I'm *bonded*," he said finally.

I moved through the water until I could put my arms around him.

"Do you regret it?" I asked.

He shook his head at once.

"No, but all of these feelings are unexpected."

He searched my eyes.

"And good," he added.

Bending to press his lips to mine, he moaned softly.

"I guess the only problem is that now that I can have you all the time, I am never going to get anything done."

I grinned against his lips, kissing him again. Keeping it light in case the kissing set us off again.

We managed to keep our hands mostly off each other as we carried on with our day. There was a light breakfast set out in the main hall, and of course, everyone wanted to know about our night.

Just before it was time to pack up and descend, Latif sat up and looked around at everyone there.

"Oh," he said. "Where is Addy?"

His al-mother laughed.

"It took this long for you to notice he isn't here?" she demanded.

Latif frowned, exchanging a glance with me, clearly sharing my thoughts. After what had happened in the library, maybe he wasn't very happy that I had won Latif in the auction.

The descent from Mount Ethos wasn't nearly as fun as going up, especially since my legs were a little worn out from the day before.

But getting back down to the city, walking with my new partner at my side, his hand in mine, everything felt different.

"You may, of course, have your assigned house back," Kion informed me. "It is now yours permanently, for you and your family."

My family.

Our conversation from last night came back to mind and me and Latif exchanged a look.

"I want to go pack my things," Latif said.

"Stop being so eager to leave," his om-father said from behind us, smacking his arm lightly. "Let me enjoy having your room as it is for a few more days."

Latif chuckled.

"Fine, you can pretend I'm at the temple while Blaine shows me to our new home."

He tugged me away from the group as everyone began to go in their own directions.

When we reached the black curtains in my door, I stopped Latif from entering.

"We're going to do *this* part the human way," I said and, without warning, hoisted him up into my arms, bridal style.

Latif laughed, throwing his arms around my neck.

"What are you doing?"

"Carrying you across the threshold," I huffed. "For luck."

I had forgotten to open the curtain first so tried unsuccessfully to kick it out of the way and then gave up and just walked us through it while Latif cackled.

We had to go halfway into the room before it fell from our heads.

"Humans are odd," Latif informed me, still laughing.

"Ain't that the truth," I chuckled, then dragged him through each room.

"This is the living room," I said. "Kitchen, bedroom, washroom, window."

He laughed, pulling me to a stop and hugging me.

"Has it been enough time to start making love again?"

I only hoped I was able to properly keep up with Latif now that there was nothing stopping us. There was no way I could say no to him.

In answer, I hoisted him up in my arms and carried him to the bed, falling onto it with him under me.

When we were done, a while later, I was starving, and it looked like the sky outside the window was starting to darken.

Latif sighed happily, squeezing me. He pressed his nose to my neck, inhaling and snuggling in.

"Your scent is so soothing," he whispered. "I don't even want to move until at least morning."

I chuckled, holding him tightly to my chest but not immediately saying yes. He pulled back to look at me.

"What's wrong?" he demanded.

"Nothing," I said, kissing his cheek. "I just thought we should probably check on Alex and maybe get some food."

"Of course," he said softly but didn't move. "Why *did* you want to take Alex away so much? Were you truly just friends before?"

I smiled softly.

"No, we never had that kind of relationship. He was my friend, and I was his mentor too," I explained. "I guess I've been too overprotective of him."

He hummed.

"I do understand not wanting to leave an unmated omega here, but he *is* mated, and Saar is good to him from what I have seen."

I nodded.

"I'm starting to see that now."

Smiling, he pushed himself up, climbing out of bed.

"Let us go check on him. This pregnancy has been hard on him."

We got dressed quickly before heading to their place. Latif knew the way, which was lucky since I hadn't been there yet.

At the front entrance, Latif simply called inside.

"Hello? Is anyone home?"

After a moment, Saar pulled the curtain open.

He watched us for a moment and then gave me the warmest smile I had ever seen from him.

"Blaine," he said. "Of course you would arrive now. And with your new mate so too. Alex will be so happy."

Saar stepped aside, allowing us room to enter, then led us through the house to the bedroom.

I heard the baby's gurgling just before we entered and stepped into the room to find Alex propped up in bed with his child in his arms. He was looking down at it with wet eyes and a happy, tired smile, but at our entrance, his gaze flew up to us and the tears started pouring in a fresh wave.

"Blaine," he laughed. "It's so good to have an old friend here to be with us. Look."

I came forward, moved, and sat gently on the edge of the bed next to him, staring mesmerized at the infant he held.

It was smaller than I'd expected it to be, and its

body was still swollen and pink from being inside Alex. The small, round face looked very human, as did the rest of it.

"Here," Alex whispered.

He handed the baby to me with such gentleness that I was afraid to take it.

To my surprise, a tiny, yellow tail wrapped around my arm and the little hands searched the air for a moment before settling back down.

"A girl," Alex said softly. "An omega."

I stared down at the small face, unable to look away.

"I'm going to be the best uncle in the world," I promised.

Saar squeezed my shoulder, and I looked over at him.

"Congratulations," I told him. "She's beautiful."

On my other side, Latif leaned against my shoulder, offering the baby his finger. She gripped it instinctively and I felt him melt a little.

"She's so sweet," he said smiling. "And so, so *small*."

"Much smaller than a fully nassa baby," Alex agreed. "Which I'm glad for, since she nearly killed me coming out."

I reached out and squeezed Alex's arm.

"Was it bad?"

"Yeah, to be honest, it hurt a lot and I got a tear down there." He grimaced. "But it was fast, and the doctors here work miracles, so I'm sure I'll be fine."

"He was so strong," Saar said, stroking back his hair.

"Does she have a name?" Latif asked.

"Aurora," Alex said.

"A human name," I said, surprised.

"Yes," Saar said. "And from the stars. So that she always remembers where she came from."

I looked down at her. At the soft yellow fuzz on her head and yellow scales and tail. Half human, half nassa. And an omega. I wondered what her life would be like.

Good, I decided. Because she had family and friends that already loved her. And anyway, I doubted that Latif was done making the world a better place yet.

I looked at him, overwhelmed by the love that had come over me, so swift and all-encompassing that my life would be forever changed.

And I had never been so grateful to be given a gift as I was to have been given all of *this*.

No matter what else life had in store, at Latif's side was where I would be.

twenty

. . .

LATIF

Life was a strange thing.

Before Blaine had walked into my fighting class, nothing had mattered to me more than learning the next move and finding my own freedom.

Now I watched Blaine holding the small half-human infant and something stirred inside me.

When she began to cry, Saar reached for her.

The moment she settled into his large arms, she made a small, satisfied gurgle and settled down.

We all giggled.

"Too cute," Alex said. "Look at how much she loves her daddy already."

"She can tell from my scent," Saar said gently, "that I am here to protect her forever. Right, little one?"

The way he looked at her made my chest ache.

Alex reached out, squeezing his arm lovingly.

It was surreal that only a couple of days ago Blaine had been threatening to take him away. Now here Blaine was, mated to me, and Alex and Saar were happy with their new baby. Life truly was mysterious.

"Can we do anything to help?" Blaine asked.

They both shook their heads.

"Saar's parents are taking care of everything we need," Alex said.

"But come by whenever you are able to visit Alex," Saar added. "That is the whole reason he made you come here, after all."

"Really?" I asked, surprised.

Alex shrugged, his cheeks turning pink.

"I wanted a friend around while I was having my baby," he said. "Can you blame me?"

I smiled warmly.

"I cannot. And I am so glad that you convinced him."

"You two are a match made in the stars." He winked. "Who knew."

Blaine shook his head in wonder, catching my gaze.

My heart squeezed at the look in his eyes.

"Let's give these two their privacy," he suggested. I nodded, allowing him to take my hand and lead me out again.

"She is so sweet," I said the moment we were outside.

"I agree wholeheartedly," Blaine said, his gaze lingering on me again. "She makes me think it might not be such a bad thing if you do end up pregnant from our carelessness."

"Would you truly want that?" I asked carefully. "Because I never thought of myself having a child before."

"We don't have to."

"I know," I said. "But I have this overwhelming feeling now that we should."

He raised his brows, stepping up to put his arms around my waist.

"Really?" he asked.

"Yes," I said nodding. "I did not think I would ever be bonded before either, but now I've come to realize it was not because I did not want to have a mate. I just wanted to be given the same respect and consideration that an alpha is given."

He nodded his agreement.

"You will not stop me from bettering the lives of omegas on Mukhana. In fact, you helped me unwittingly to show how strong I truly am... A baby would not stop me either."

"Well, you know I'm not going anywhere. You don't have to decide now."

I smiled, squeezing him.

"I know, but I think... it might be nice."

He tugged me down, pressing our lips together before responding.

"I get it," he finally said. "At this point in life, I thought the idea of having a family was behind me. Now it seems like it could be a reality, and... yeah. It does sound nice, doesn't it?"

"We can practice with Aurora first," I suggested, and he laughed.

"Good idea. Maybe we should start small. Babysitting should ease us into it."

"Oh! Blaine, Latif, you are here already."

Together, we turned to find Head Alpha Kion approaching, a smile on his lips.

"You two seem to be settling into the bonded life with ease," he noted.

I nodded.

"Yes, Head Alpha," I agreed. "And congratulations, Aurora is beautiful."

His smile grew bright, gold eyes glittering.

"Isn't she the most beautiful baby?" he asked. "My granddaughter is one of a kind."

He eyed us.

"Unless, of course, you decide to have a child too. I am now certain that the half-human ones are the sweetest of them all."

We glanced at each other, and he must have read the look, because he patted us both on the shoulders as though it was already decided.

"Very good," he said.

He turned to enter his son's home but paused and turned back to us.

"Latif, now that the celebration is done, we must discuss what happened at the auction."

"Oh, of course," I said, instantly nervous.

"Tomorrow," he said. "With the whole council present."

He waited for me to nod and then patted my shoulder again in passing, going inside.

"It'll be fine," Blaine said at once. "There's nothing to be nervous about. We're already bonded."

That *did* instantly soothe me.

"You don't believe he wants to punish me?" I asked.

He shook his head at once, beginning to pull me down the street.

"He didn't seem angry," Blaine said. "More curious. Maybe they want to learn your moves or something."

I snorted.

"Then they should go to Devin for that."

And sure enough, they did, because when we entered the council building the next morning after being summoned, Devin was there, seated at the table with the rest of the council.

I was still a little bit nervous even though Blaine had done his best to distract me until now, but like when I'd jumped into the pit to fight for Blaine, a calm settled over me as we took our seats.

Devin gave me a curious shrug, indicating that he didn't know what this was about either. Clearly, Eisa had not yet let him in on the secret.

"There will be plenty of time to chat later," Head Alpha Kion said. "So let us begin straight away. Alya?"

She nodded and faced me, looking straight into my eyes.

"Latif," she started, "what you did at the auction... We are all very impressed by it."

Stunned, I stared at her for a moment while her words penetrated.

"You were?"

"Yes, and many others were as well."

"We have been inundated with requests from the families of unmated omegas," Head Alpha Kion said.

"Requests for what?" I asked slowly.

"For training, first and foremost," Eisa said proudly.

His arm went around Devin's shoulders, pulling him into a quick embrace.

"Also for leniency in other areas," Alya said. "So, we have come to a decision on behalf of the citizens of Mukhana and Diwan in particular."

My heart started to pound.

"Our society has been in need of change for some time. The number of omegas being born has dwindled and instinctively, as alphas, we became more protective," Alya was saying. "Now, you have shown us that it is time to release the hold we have over you all."

Disbelief filled me.

"You can't mean..."

I swallowed and looked around the room at each of their faces, seeing the truth in everyone.

"Are you freeing the unmated omegas?" I asked.

"With restrictions," Alya agreed. "First, we require that the omega can fight like you."

My gaze caught Devin's across the table.

"With all due respect, Latif is my best fighter. He submitted fifteen alphas and barely lost his breath.

There's no need for every omega to reach his level before being allowed to walk down the street."

The alphas in the room shared a silent look.

"That is why we have brought you here," Head Alpha Kion finally said. "We would like you and Latif to create a system to measure by. And of course, we must see their progress before approving them."

"And what about the alphas?" I found myself asking.

I caught Blaine stifling a proud smile and that pushed me to keep going.

"What about the alphas?" Eisa asked.

He only looked curious but, considering that not long ago he had broken into a human ship to steal an omega, I could not help but use him as an example.

"Omegas go to great lengths to learn self-control," I said. "Yet alphas are weak enough to steal omegas when they want one. They should be required to put in as much training as omegas do in order for both to coexist unmated."

To his credit, Eisa did not look angry, only thoughtful, although he did shoot Devin a look, to which his mate only smiled and patted his arm.

"He is right, of course," Devin said, winking at me.

The rest of the council was quiet.

"Then perhaps this program reaches beyond the

omegas. We shall need to create a new curriculum for all those who are unmated... Of course, we will need help from omegas to deem what is most important."

They were all watching me, seemingly waiting for a response. I could hardly believe it, but ideas were already formulating in my mind.

"I know just what to do," I said confidently.

Satisfied, Head Alpha Kion turned to Blaine.

"Are you opposed to Latif working on this project with us?"

Blaine smiled at the question, bemused, and glanced at me. I could tell in the fleeting look that he was amazed by how little the alphas here got it.

"I support anything that Latif wants to do," he said, then reached out, taking my hand and meeting my eyes properly this time.

"It's not up to me," he said gently. "From now on, everything in your life is in your hands. And I'll be right there with you, supporting you the whole way."

"Very well then. We will begin to make arrangements at once," Head Alpha Kion was saying, but I couldn't look at him.

And despite the importance of the moment, I couldn't hear them anymore.

I was far too distracted by the human at my side

who had unexpectedly come into my life to change everything.

All this time I'd wanted to do everything on my own, but being with Blaine didn't feel like it took anything away from me. Instead, for the first time, I had support.

As the meeting ended, and we stood to leave, Devin came and gave me a quick hug, patting my back.

"You've made me a proud man," he said.

"It was because of you," I mumbled as happiness filled me.

He shook his head.

"No, you're the one who showed everyone without a doubt that the omegas can hold their own."

Pride swelled in me.

"Thank you," I said.

Outside, walking back toward our house, I still couldn't believe it.

"The alpha council is more understanding than I thought," I mused. "I assumed it would take a lot longer to get to this point."

Blaine hummed thoughtfully.

"I guess alphas aren't all bad," he joked, bumping his shoulder to mine.

"I suppose not," I agreed, nudging him back. "At

least this one is changing my mind."

He grinned and pulled me to a stop.

I hadn't noticed that we had reached the town fountain until he was leading me to sit on the edge, listening to the water flow.

Taking my hands in his, he rubbed his thumb over my knuckles, his eyes looking straight through me in the way they always had.

"Do you have any plans for how to teach the alphas some self-control?" he asked.

I couldn't help but smile because the idea of them finally having to learn the same things as the omegas was incredibly satisfying.

"We use meditation, mostly," I said. "I think that would be the best way... although Naz teaches the omegas. I wonder if he would be comfortable to teach the alphas too."

"Is that even allowed?" Blaine asked. "I thought he wasn't even supposed to interact with alphas."

"True," I agreed, "but so much is about to change. Maybe that will too."

Blaine shook his head.

"Were you always so inspiring?" he asked.

I chuckled.

"Until you came around, all anyone ever thought I was, was defiant."

He grinned.

"Trailblazers always are."

"Trailblazers?" I repeated.

"It's a human term used to describe someone who burns up a new path for others to follow," he explained. "And it's the best word to describe you, my passionate, unstoppable, incredible, Latif."

My chest tightened.

For a moment I had to look away as the reality of everything that had happened filled me.

Somehow, the universe had decided to give me everything that I had wanted and then some. It had delivered my other half from a planet far away... Of course, it made sense now that only someone from another world could truly understand me. Still, it was humbling to know that I hadn't known *every-thing* that I wanted.

"What is it?" Blaine asked gently.

I shrugged helplessly.

"I'm just wondering how I ever got so lucky."

"You worked for it," Blaine said firmly. "Don't forget that."

I shook my head, smiling faintly.

"Not for you," I whispered. "In fact, I fought *against* getting a mate. But it seems the universe knew better."

He smiled and I could *feel* the warmth and love in his eyes.

"And I hadn't been planning on staying here, but I guess you can't stop fate."

"No," I agreed. "Not from setting *us* together."

It seemed we were two *trailblazers* from different worlds, meant to collide.

Blaine leaned closer, pressing his soft lips to mine, instantly making my stomach swoop.

"I can't wait to see what else fate has in store for us," he said, pulling back just far enough to speak. "I know we can handle anything."

"Together," I agreed.

And now I knew, whatever road I traveled in life, Blaine would be walking with me, his hand in mine. Always.

END

afterword

Thank you for reading Blaine and Latif's story!

If you want to read the next book, which will be Addy's story, you can preorder it on Amazon here: books2read.com/CovetedOmega or, you can get early access and read as I'm writing it on my Ream! https://reamstories.com/siennasway

It's hard to believe that I've finished three Alien's Omega books plus a novella! It's been so cool to learn more about this world. I have so many more ideas. Maybe you noticed me introducing a few new characters. The current plan is to write at least three more books.

As much as I adore Blaine and Latif, and couldn't wait to get to them, finishing this book took pure grit and determination because everything in life seemed to be getting in the way. Luckily I had great support from my fiancé who stepped up so I could lock myself in the office for hours at a time. I also had the help of my friend and editor Ashley, who was willing to read as I was writing. They are the reason that I was able to write the book that I wanted. Thank you!

I'm so proud of this one and I hope you can feel all the love in these pages.

about the author

Sienna Sway is a Canadian with her head up in the clouds. Books and writing M/M are her lifelong passions. She has always adored scifi and fantasy and is currently living her dream by writing these books. Thank you for your support!

Join her newsletter for monthly m/m recs and updates, or follow her at any of the links below!

Newsletter: http://eepurl.com/g-E50H
Website: www.siennasway.com
Ream: https://reamstories.com/siennasway
FB group: www.facebook.com/groups/
outofthisworldmm/
Instagram and X/twitter: @siennasway
TikTok: @siennaswayauthor

also by sienna sway

THE MISMATCHED PRINCES

The Oaf's Prince

The Elf's Prince

The Wolf's Prince

THE ALIEN'S OMEGA

The Alien's Kidnapped Omega

The Alien's Runaway Omega

The Alien's Pregnant Omega

The Alien's Defiant Omega

The Alien's Coveted Omega

TETHERED SOULS

Tethered Souls

Tethered Desire

LUNAR CITY FIGHT LEAGUE

Bait Wolf

Shifting Alphas

www.ingramcontent.com/pod-product-compliance
Lightning Source LLC
Chambersburg PA
CBHW060545180626
46817CB00002B/727